TOPAZ

Other Books by the Same Author

Beau Barron's Lady
Regency Rogue
The Michaelmas Tree
The Loving Highwayman

The Regency Jewel Series

Emerald
Sapphire
Pearl
Garnet
Ruby
Opal

TOPAZ

Helen Ashfield

A THOMAS DUNNE BOOK

St. Martin's Press
New York

Library of Congress Cataloging-in-Publication Data

Bennetts, Pamela.
Topaz.

"A Thomas Dunne book."
I. Title.
PR6052.E533T6 1987 823'.914 87-1686
ISBN 0-312-00695-0

First published in Great Britain by Robert Hale Limited.

First U.S. Edition

10 9 8 7 6 5 4 3 2 1

Acknowledgments

I would like to express my gratitude to the authors of the following books which not only provided me with the information I needed, but also gave me much pleasure when I read them. Without such help, this novel could not have been written:

Gypsies of Britain, Brian Vesey-FitzGerald
Gipsies – A Mysterious People, Charles Duff
In the Life of a Romany Gypsy, Manfri Frederick Wood
Portrait of Dartmoor, Vian Smith
Worth's Dartmoor, Compiled from the published works of R. Hansford Worth
Dartmoor Villages, S.H. Burton
Portrait of Devon, D. St. Leger-Gordon
Leisure and Pleasure in the Nineteenth Century, Stella Margetson
The Age of Elegance, Arthur Bryant
Regency Roundabout, Dorothy Margaret Stuart
The Regency Costume and Fashion 1760-1920, Jack Cassin-Scott
The Fashionable Lady in the 19th Century, Charles H. Gibbs-Smith
19th-Century Costume, Victoria and Albert Museum – Introduction by James Laver
Handbook of English Costume in the 19th Century, C. Willett Cunnington and Phillis Cunnington

P.B.

One

Dartmoor: 1807

The gypsies arrived on Dartmoor early that year. They came in a long winding string of wagons, horses, barking dogs, dancing children and donkeys. The women wore coloured skirts down to their ankles, their earrings and beads jangling as they moved with sinuous grace over the uneven ground. Ahead of them, as was fitting, were the menfolk, more soberly-clad save for the bright kerchiefs round their necks.

They always camped at Dartmeet in summer. It was the place where the rivers of the East and West Dart met before rushing down, full-blown, to Totnes. Above, Yar Tor frowned down upon the intrusion, but the travellers didn't notice. They were never welcome wherever they went and they had grown used to the Moor.

They were not overawed by the forbidding tors and jagged rocks, nor felt themselves threatened by the rolling acres of granite uplands. They scarcely noticed the occasional ravine and were careful to avoid the mires and blanket bogs laid down by Nature to trap the unwary.

The sudden gathering overhead of ominous clouds left them unmoved, although they shewed a healthy respect for the mists which could appear in seconds to blot out everything in sight.

There were seven families in all; the Prices, the Ingrams, the Pinfolds, the Roberts, the Burtons, the Coopers and the Chilcotts. They were proud people jealous of their lineage, scorning those not of pure Romany blood.

Topaz Chilcott walked behind her family, hanging back a little as if to emphasise the fact that she had never really been accepted by it. She was a posh-rat, the offspring of a Romany and a *gaujo,* or non-gypsy, and she was never allowed to forget it.

Her mother, Lavender, had fallen in love with a scholarly man called Frederick Legh when she had met him walking on the Moor. She had run away with him to London where she had borne him a daughter, naming her Topaz after a jewel her lover had given her. Three weeks later Lavender had died of puerperal fever, but long before that Legh had come to his senses. The romantic interlude had withered very rapidly once he was back in town.

He hadn't wanted an illegitimate child cluttering up his life, particularly when a rich widow had started to cast meaningful glances in his direction. He had returned to Dartmoor when he knew the tribes would be there, begging them to take Topaz off his hands. He had farmed the child out, of course, but he hadn't been able to quell the fear that somehow she might intrude upon his future.

Legh offered twenty pounds, the gem which his dead mistress had prized so much, and some gold earrings, saying that the infant was to be called Topaz. It was of no interest to Loverin, Topaz's uncle and head of the family, what name the girl had been given. He pocketed the money, whilst Liti, his wife, appropriated the jewel on its fine gold chain.

Had Legh but known it, he could have saved his bribes. Loverin couldn't turn Topaz away. She was Amossy Chilcott's granddaughter and, whatever the circumstances, that fact could not be ignored. The old man had been revered during his lifetime and even more so after his death. The Chilcotts were still commonly known as Amossy's tribe, his shade an ever-present influence upon them.

Topaz had Amossy's fierce, unyielding spirit and hadn't been broken by the indifference and contempt shewn to her since she was old enough to understand such treatment.

She had always been given the most unpleasant tasks to perform, punished when she rebelled, as often she did, growing up without knowledge of love or hearing the sound of a kind word.

People said that she was as wild as the Moor itself and just as changeable. One moment she could be smiling tenderly as she fed the animals, the next filled with anger and as dangerous as a tiger at bay. She was always the outsider, refusing to conform to traditions, obstinate and impudent. It was the way she hid the hurt inside herself, too proud to shew one iota of what she was feeling.

In summer, such free time as she had was spent on the Moor. She loved it and wished she could stay there forever. It was untamed, like herself, and she was in tune with its every mood. Many of the people in the villages on the fringe of Dartmoor were afraid of what lay at the heart of the upland. Topaz understood their fear without sharing it. There was something brooding and menacing about it, unseen, but felt by many. It excited her and she promised herself that one day she would unravel the mystery.

She had inherited from her father a quick, enquiring mind and was hungry for knowledge beyond the skills possessed by the Romanies. They couldn't read or write, but Topaz longed to do both and more besides. She wanted to know about the world in which she lived, learn about strange lands beyond the seas, and the even more puzzling ways of the *gaujos* who spent their whole time shut up in houses made of bricks or stone, as if they had condemned themselves to perpetual imprisonment.

That morning her spirits were low. She was sixteen and of marriagable age. Her uncle and aunt had decided it was time she took a husband, their choice for her being Manfro Draper, a posh-rat like herself. He was nineteen, not uncomely, and Topaz disliked him most heartily.

She had refused flatly to consider him as her groom, but the time of reckoning was at hand. For once, Chilcott had kept his temper, hoping to coax his niece round to his point of view. When it became clear that she was adamantly opposed to his suggestion, he had decreed that upon reaching Dartmeet all her nonsense must stop. There would be a wedding whether she liked it or not.

When Manfro detached himself from the other men and came to walk by her side, Topaz glared at him.

"What do you want?"

Draper moistened his lips. It wasn't only Chilcott's promise of a tidy sum of money and six horses if he would take Topaz as his spouse which made Manfro want her.

She was a beauty and he'd often wanted to steal a kiss, but had had enough sense not to try. Gypsy women were chaste before wedlock and Chilcott might have called off the arrangement if he got to hear of such liberties being taken.

"Just wanted to talk to you. No harm in that, is there?"

"I don't want to talk to you, so go away."

"No need to be like this. Why don't you say yes? It 'ud please your aunt and uncle and we'd do well enough together."

Topaz gave him a withering glance.

"You might do well enough, but I wouldn't. I've seen you beat the horses cruelly and kick the dogs out of your way. You'd do the same to me if I were your wife."

"I swear I wouldn't."

"You're a liar and a thief, too."

He went fiery red, hands clenched at his sides.

"Thief? What d'yer mean? I never stole nothing."

Topaz gave a short laugh.

"Yes you did. I saw you take money from Nixi Pinfold's jacket yesterday. He left it lying on the ground and you thought no one was about. But I was. I'd rather bed with the Devil than you, so go about your business and leave me alone."

"Your uncle'll make you obey." Manfro's temper was ragged because she'd seen his pilfering. "They want you out of the way."

"Maybe, but they won't get rid of me by making me clasp hands with you. I don't want you near me. You smell."

Draper slouched away, swearing under his breath as Topaz braced herself for battle with Loverin and Liti. She had been dismissive enough with Manfro, but she wasn't quite sure how she was going to get out of her predicament. She hadn't a penny piece with which to bless herself and few skills. No one employed travellers if they could help it and the future looked dark.

Then she squared her shoulders, remembering she was Amossy's kin. Whatever happened, she wouldn't let her determination waver over the rejection of the abominable Draper.

Later that morning her uncle and aunt sent for her. She walked over to them, her chin up. Aunt Liti had a nut-brown face, hard black eyes and a hook of a nose. She was particular about her appearance, boasting more clothes and jewellery than any other female in the tribe. That, she considered, was as it should be, seeing she was Loverin's wife. She wielded great power among the women, most of whom were afraid of her. She looked up from her Tarot cards as Topaz approached, her thin lips tightening.

From the beginning she had been angered at having to take the girl in, for Lavender had been lovely, and Liti detested her for it. She detested Topaz for exactly the same reason and her constant nagging had made Loverin's mind up for him.

Loverin tried to be jovial, still hoping to get his niece's agreement without a lot of argument.

"You've had time to think over what your aunt and me have said. You'll have to marry sometime and you'll never get a better offer than this. Manfro's a good man."

Topaz flicked a look at her intended. He was lounging against a post, clad in his best suit, undressing her with his eyes.

"Manfro is a bully, a liar and a thief," she said, her brief survey finished. "I couldn't have a worse offer if I lived to be a hundred. Nothing will make me change my mind. I won't have him."

Chilcott's veneer of good-humour vanished instantly and his brow was thunderous.

"You ungrateful bitch!"

"That you are." Liti joined in, strident and condemning. "Didn't your uncle and me take you in even though you were tainted? Haven't we and the whole family done everything for you?"

Topaz's eyes smouldered as they met her aunt's.

"You've done some things for me. You've given me enough food to keep me alive and Cousin Genti's cast-off clothing, seeing we're the same size. But you've worked me harder than any donkey and you've let Tom, Amos and Oseri bait me as if I were a chained bear."

Liti screamed her outrage.

"There! Do you hear her? My sons are decent boys and you've no call to complain where they're concerned. And where would you be without us I'd like to know? We've suffered the shame of your mother's whoring and this is all the thanks we get."

"She wasn't a whore!" Topaz stamped her foot, beside herself with fury as she tried to defend the dead woman whose legacy she had to bear. "I won't listen to you. I know she must have loved my father and he her."

"Ah, but he didn't marry her, did he?" Liti pounced triumphantly. "She was a harlot right enough. She'd lift her skirts for any man."

"I hate you!" Topaz took a step forwards and in spite of her superior position, Liti drew back in alarm. "I loathe you because you're still jealous of her. Everyone said how pretty she was, not like you with your crooked nose and wrinkled skin – "

"Hold your tongue!" Loverin hissed the words out, his face puce. It wasn't only the thought of what Liti would be like when they were alone. This hot-tempered ingrate was denying him his rights as head of the tribe. "I'm not standing here all day bickering about this. My mind's made up. To-night you marry Manfro Draper and to-morrow you'll be on your way and good riddance."

"I won't do it. I've told you a dozen times – I won't have him."

"Then if you won't take him willingly you can take him the other way. You'll be trussed to that post yonder and later I'll have a promise from you, even if I have to whip you raw to get it. Amos, Tom, Oseri, come and help me. Get this ungrateful cow tied up tight. Let everyone see what she is, if they don't already know. If she wants public disgrace she can have it."

A small crowd had gathered round, buzzing with the excitement which was breaking the dull monotony of the day. People parted respectfully to let the Chilcott boys pass, nodding and murmuring their approval. Topaz Chilcott had always thought too much of herself. Too stuck-up, considering what she was. The women put their heads together and agreed that it would be no bad thing if Loverin laid on hard with his strap.

Topaz knew it was then or never. Once her cousins got hold of her and she was imprisoned by ropes, nothing could save her.

She turned and ran, knocking into the bystanders as she went, not even noticing them. Her cousins could run fast, but she knew she could run faster. She'd done it before and she could do it again, especially as so much was at stake. She heard the boys hurling abuse at her, shouting to her to stop, but she shut her ears to them.

Her breath was tearing at her throat, the stitch in her side was like a knife, but still she raced on. When she couldn't take another step she turned and looked behind her. There was no sign of her pursuers and their voices had faded away. She sank down, hugging her sides, praying that Tom, Amos and Oseri wouldn't suddenly appear from behind a boulder or a fold in the hillside. When it was obvious that she was alone she got to her feet.

Her cousins had lost her and she was free. There would be no Manfro Draper and no wedding. Then she pulled a rueful face. There would be no food either, nor place to lay her head when it grew dark. Only the unfeeling Moor was left to succour her and she gritted her teeth as she began to climb a rocky incline, refusing to think about the future.

She had made her decision. Now she had to live with it.

* * *

The day after Topaz ran away, Andrew Manners, Marquis of Rossmayne, and the Hon. Timothy Amsterdam went riding early.

Both men loved Dartmoor, never happier than when the London season was over and they could return to the remote places which they had shared since childhood. They often rode for hours in contented silence, remembering the good years behind them when everything had been simple and summer seemed to last forever.

One look at the marquis told Amsterdam it was another bad day for his friend. Rossmayne was tall, with a lithe, graceful strength. Nature had touched his face with beauty, giving him finely-sculptured bones beneath a lightly tanned skin, eyes like aquamarines, and hair more silver than gold which curled slightly beneath his tall beaver hat.

Nature, however, was not responsible for the hard line of his mouth, nor the bleakness of his expression. Living with Horatia, Lord Cronmore's daughter, for three years had brought that about.

As they dismounted and tethered their horses to a clump of stunted trees, Timothy said tentatively:

"A difficult night?"

"Intolerable. Let's walk, shall we? I need exercise to get the bile out of me."

"I'm sorry, Andrew. I wish there was something I could do to help."

"No one can help. It's my own fault: I shouldn't have married her."

"You did it for your father's sake. He was dying and implored you to agree to the match because he and Horatia's father were such old friends. It consoled him to know you were going to settle down and have children. Besides, she was different in those days."

"She was exactly the same as she is now, but she took the trouble to hide the fact. If she had lovers then, I didn't know about them. Now she isn't so careful. No, I'm to blame. Whatever my father asked of me I should have said no. I didn't really like her from the start, never mind feeling any love for her. It was bound to end like this."

"If men only married women they loved, the population of England would soon dwindle to nothing. Don't judge yourself so harshly. You had no way of knowing what it would be like and she may change one day."

The marquis's lips turned down at the corners. It made him sick to go to Horatia's bed, but he hadn't shirked the task. Yet despite his efforts, his wife shewed no sign of becoming pregnant and his need for a son remained unfulfilled.

At her most vicious, Horatia would taunt him, calling into question his virility. Mostly he walked away from her jibes. Now and then, because he was a mere mortal, he would lose his temper. The previous evening had been one such occasion, their quarrel more heated than usual. It had ended when he knocked her to the ground and slammed out of the room, hearing her laughter following him down the corridor.

"She won't change," he said finally, "unless it's for the worse. And if I do get an heir it will be by accident. You're lucky, Timothy. You don't have to keep your family's name alive, and you've got me as an object lesson when you are considering matrimony."

Amsterdam nodded. He was a quiet, kindly man, with hazel eyes, a high-bridged nose and a gentle mouth. He wasn't as tall as the marquis, but he had a wiry physique and a sound constitution. When he wasn't in London, he shared an old house near Camber Tor with his aunt, Lady Agatha Waring. She was sharp-eyed and even sharper of tongue, but the bond of affection between them was unbreakable. After a season of the haut monde's artificial hypocrisy, Aunt Ag's astringent comments were a welcome relief.

"Yes, I suppose I am fortunate. But my bride, if ever I find one, will have to be a model of virtue, be possessed of the looks of Venus di Milo, and blessed with the disposition of a saint. Otherwise, Aunt Ag. won't have anything to do with her. I doubt if such a paragon exists."

"So do I. Take my advice and stay single."

Timothy was about to change what was clearly an unwelcome subject when he happened to look up, his brows meeting sharply.

"Andrew! Someone's making off with Nero."

The marquis swung round. Nero was his favourite mount and no one else was ever allowed to ride him. The animal needed careful handling and had cost a fortune.

"It's one of those bloody gypsies." Andrew bared his teeth. "They're always stealing something or other and they've got a good eye for a thoroughbred."

"It looks like a woman."

"I don't care who it is. I'll wring her neck when I lay hands on her."

They ran, covering the ground in long strides. When they reached the trees, Andrew leapt into the saddle of Amsterdam's horse and turned its head.

"Wait for me here. I'll come back to you."

"With two horses, I hope."

The marquis didn't hear Timothy. He was too intent on catching the female rogue who had taken his grey.

When Topaz had first seen the two men riding close to where she was lying behind some rocks, the idea of appropriating one of the horses hadn't occurred to her. She had never before taken anything which didn't belong to her, but she was cold, tired, and very hungry.

As she watched the strangers dismount the thought came to her. She could borrow the grey, using its strength to get her to the nearest village. There she might find someone who didn't mind employing a traveller to clean out a stable or a pig-sty, or perhaps a kindly old woman might give her a crust. The horse could be left at the local inn and its owner would soon come looking for it. In any event, such a fine beast was probably well-known in those parts.

She had hoped to get away unseen but, as she urged Nero on, a backward glance shewed that the men had spotted her. She dug her heels in as hard as she could, realizing that a rider was after her, but for all her efforts the pounding of hooves was growing nearer and nearer.

She was about to veer in a different direction when she felt an arm like steel round her waist. A second later she had fallen to the ground, her hair covering her eyes so that she had only a vague impression of the man bending over her.

She knew at once what he meant to do, for Aunt Liti had given the girls in camp enough warnings about the local gentry. 'They'll rape you as soon as look at you,' she had said. 'And they'll laugh as they ruin you.'

Topaz didn't whimper or plead. Instead, she began to fight like a wild cat. The marquis swore as she scratched his cheek, slapping her across the face with the back of his hand. If he had thought to subdue her that way, he was disappointed. He felt her teeth sink into his wrist and cursed again.

"Damn you, you slut! Stop it, stop it!"

But Topaz had no intention of stopping. She punched Rossmayne in the eye and then on the chest, tugging at his cravat until he lost his balance and fell on top of her. They rolled over and over on the damp moss, exchanging blows and vile words until finally Topaz's strength ran out.

The marquis pinned her to the ground by her shoulders, sitting astride her so that she couldn't move. It was then that she really saw him for the first time and the blood began to sing in her ears.

He was the most handsome man she had ever seen,

although his face was marred by the marks of her nails, and by bruises which would soon turn black and blue. She had never felt such a queer sensation before and was suddenly sad because it was this man who was going to take her innocence away from her.

At almost the same time, Rossmayne's blinding rage lifted long enough for him to see what sort of woman had resisted him so resolutely. He knew it was a moment he would never forget, for in that brief space of time his world changed.

He could see sorrow in the dark eyes which glowed as if there were candles burning behind them. The red lips drooped and, absurdly, he wanted to bend and kiss them. Her skin was covered with dirt, but it didn't hide its quality. He'd always thought of gypsies as swarthy of complexion, but this girl's face was pale olive and he knew that if he touched it, it would be as soft as silk. Where he had torn the dress from her shoulders the gentle swell of one breast gave promise of the advent of rich womanhood and he longed to cup it in his hand so that its sweet warmth rested against his own flesh.

Slowly his hold slackened and he rose to his feet, his fine frilled shirt ripped to pieces by her long, slender fingers, his expensive riding habit covered in mud.

"By Christ, madam, what are you? A female pugilist?" He had to make mock of her because otherwise he would have knelt down again and cradled her close to him to comfort her. "I swear you'd make a worthy opponent in any ring. Now get up. You and I have an appointment with the local magistrate."

He understood why she didn't move. The same kind of inertia had held him prisoner a few seconds before, but common sense made him brush his nonsensical thoughts aside.

He pulled her to her feet, marvelling that so slight a creature could have put up such a fight. He wished he could go on holding her hand, but that was impossible.

"I meant no harm," she said and brushed the hair from her forehead. "I was only borrowing your horse."

For a moment Andrew was diverted again. The sheen on the long hair quickened his desire and the music in her voice surprised him. When she had been wrestling with him she had used the foul language common among gypsies. Now she looked almost like a child about to be scolded for some minor misdemeanour.

"Borrowing him? Do you really expect me to believe that?" Andrew pushed her away from him because by then he had realised the danger she posed. "Don't add lies to horse-theft. If you do, the law will deal with you with even greater severity."

"I wasn't lying. I truly did mean just to ride him to the nearest hamlet. I've been on the Moor all night, you see. I was cold and hungry and I – "

The marquis frowned. The thought of the girl being hungry was insupportable and then he noticed how thin her torn garment was and how deep the hollows beneath her cheekbones. She had been neglected and he ached because of it, but it wouldn't do to let her know that.

"What's your name?" he asked brusquely.

"Topaz Chilcott."

"Topaz? That isn't a proper name."

"It was what my mother said I was to be called before she died."

"She must have had a fanciful imagination, or been delirious. Why were you on the Moor alone? Where's the rest of your family or tribe, or whatever you call it?"

"At Dartmeet, but I've run away. I'd rather face the Moor, starvation and anything else, than see Manfro Draper again. I'm sorry I hit you just now. I was sure you were going to rape me."

"Rape you? Why on earth should I do that?"

"Aunt Liti said all the gentry used Romany women that way if they get the chance."

"She was mistaken and who, pray, is Manfro Draper?"

Topaz didn't have a chance to reply because Timothy Amsterdam had walked up to them and was staring at the marquis in blank amazement.

"I got tired of waiting," he said at last. "My dear Andrew, have you any idea what a spectacle you make?"

"I've got a very good idea," returned Rossmayne with some feeling. "My dishevelled appearance is due entirely to Miss Topaz Chilcott, who imagined that I was going to have my wicked way with her. She also tells fairy stories about borrowing horses. Oh, by the way, she's hungry."

Timothy turned to look at Topaz and became strangely silent. In spite of her rags and the marquis's rough treatment, he had never seen a more entrancing girl, nor one who had affected him so instantly. He took a long breath, becoming severely practical before he got out of his depth.

"Then we'd better feed her, hadn't we? There's a village a mile or so away. No doubt we can get a meal of sorts there."

"She deserves to be in prison, not in a local hostelry eating at our expense."

Amsterdam glanced at Andrew and read at once what was in his eyes. He knew every inflection of the marquis's voice and it wasn't hard to guess what had happened. It wasn't going to help Andrew's plight, finding himself bewitched by a young gypsy girl he could never have, but Fate wasn't always kind when it selected the tricks it was going to play. He understood only too well why the marquis was so attracted to Topaz Chilcott. His own heart would never be quite the same now that he'd seen her.

"But you're not going to have her put in prison, m'dear Andrew, are you?"

The marquis shot Topaz an unfriendly look. Then he shrugged.

"No, I suppose not. It's too much trouble, but I want the whole truth about this rubbish concerning the loan of Nero. You can tell us about it over the meal."

"They won't let me inside the door of an inn." Topaz was trying to pretend that this man wasn't making her weak at the knees. "Perhaps you could hand me out some bread or something like that."

"They'll admit you if you're with me."

"I don't think so, not unless you're very important indeed."

Amsterdam laughed. She really was enchanting, very earnest as she tried to save Andrew from embarrassment.

"I see that you haven't been properly introduced," he said, "and that must be put right at once. Miss Chilcott, this is Andrew Manners, Marquis of Rossmayne. There isn't an inn, or any other eating house come to that, which would dare close its doors against him or his guests. Don't worry. He's important enough. And my name is Timothy Amsterdam – your humble servant."

When the worst of her hunger had been appeased, Topaz began to tell her story. She had meant to confine herself to the unwelcome proposal of marriage from Manfro Draper, but somehow she found herself telling her listeners all about her mother and father, Uncle Loverin and Aunt Liti, and the cousins she couldn't abide.

"You've had a hard time, Miss Chilcott."

Topaz flushed at Amsterdam's sympathy.

"I didn't mean to say so much. You must think me a terrible whiner."

"Not at all. You've had a lot to contend with and the marquis did ask to hear your tale. What are you going to do now?"

"Find work somewhere, I hope."

Timothy glanced at the marquis who was gazing out of the window, apparently deaf to the conversation. Amsterdam didn't want to upset Topaz. Indeed, the exact opposite was in his mind, but he was afraid of the further rejection she would face in any hamlet or village for miles around.

"Will that be possible?"

Topaz didn't beat about the bush.

"You mean because I'm a gypsy?"

"Yes." Timothy was equally blunt, for this was no time for dissembling. "I understand that people don't welcome them in these parts."

"Nor anywhere else, sir, but I've got to try. I've no money and nowhere to go. What can I do?"

"You can come with us to the Convent of St. Francis near Wild Tor. I know the Mother Superior; she's a good woman and will look after you."

Topaz stared at the marquis whose suggestion had left her dumbfounded.

"A convent! Oh no, I couldn't."

"You've no choice. You said yourself that you were penniless and homeless. You'll be well-cared for there; given food and a bed to lie in. I'll see if they can ram some learning into you as well."

"But you don't know what I'm like. Even my own people say I'm thoroughly bad and I've got the temper of Old Nick."

"I can testify to that." Andrew gave a thin smile. "One look at me now would convince anyone of your lack of restraint."

"I did say I was sorry. I thought – "

"Yes, yes, I know what you thought and stop apologizing. You got as good as you gave. Did I hurt you?"

The marquis's voice had softened and for the first time Topaz gave him a wide smile. Andrew felt his heart turn over and looked back at the view so that she shouldn't see what she was doing to him. He knew he was behaving ludicrously and the sooner he got the wench locked up with a pack of nuns the better.

"Not much; no more than I deserved, anyway. But a convent! They won't have me."

"We won't know that until we ask them, will we, and I doubt if they'll refuse you shelter. It's Mother Benedicta or back to Manfro Draper. I'm not leaving you on the Moor by yourself, so make up your mind which you prefer."

Again Timothy's lips moved slightly. Andrew's proposal was very correct and proper, but he doubted if his friend's thoughts were quite so pure.

"How old are you, Miss Chilcott?" he asked. "Forgive me if the question is an impertinence."

"It isn't, sir. I'm sixteen, and no one ever calls me Miss Chilcott."

"I shall do so until you give me leave to be more familiar."

"You're very kind, Mr. Amsterdam and you, too, sir."

"I'm never that; ask anybody." Andrew had turned his head, taking another look at his protegée. She had washed her hands and face at the pump in front of the inn. As he had suspected, her skin had the unmistakable radiance of youth. It made him angry again. "You're just a nuisance and I've got to find something to do with you, horse-thief though you be."

"I'm not!"

"Yes you are and don't argue with me. Well, what's it to be? Wild Tor or Manfro Draper's bed?"

That time, Topaz heard something in the marquis's voice which filled her with tremulous hope. He didn't want her to become Manfro's wife. She knew it instinctively in spite of the curtness of his words. But it was silly to dream of things which couldn't be. She mustn't let the sense of happiness grow and blossom just because she had met him. After he'd left her at Wild Tor, they would never see each other again.

"What do you want me to do?"

"I don't give a damn one way or the other."

"I'd take Mother Benedicta if I were you," advised Amsterdam, trying to dispel the sting of the marquis's response. "After all, in a few years you can leave the convent. If you go back to Draper you'll have to serve a life sentence."

"I wouldn't want that." Topaz seemed to be speaking to herself. "Especially now."

Andrew had cut himself out of the discussion once more.

There was an agony inside him which he had never felt before and he closed his eyes briefly. It was such a ridiculous situation. The Marquis of Rossmayne, married, a leader of the fashionable set, falling in love at first sight with a tinker. He didn't deny the truth to himself; there was no point.

He had had a number of mistresses and felt affection for some of them. He had no experience of deep love, but he recognized it when it struck him hard and unexpectedly. He knew it wasn't a passing thing either. For as many years as he was allotted he would remember this girl and love her.

When he heard her last remark he understood it and knew he had to get rid of her quickly. He pushed the table back impatiently and stood up.

"We must go, or it'll be dark before we know it. Here, landlord, take this. And you, madam, you can ride with me. At least that way I shall be able to stop you purloining Nero again.

"Hell's teeth! Whatever can I have done to deserve you, Miss Chilcott?"

Two

When Topaz first saw the Convent of St. Francis she was filled with panic.

"I can't stay here, not in a place with walls and a roof."

"What did you expect it to be like?" The marquis lifted her from the saddle, feeling the warmth of her body against his own, wishing he could go on holding her for ever. "It's unheard of for a religious Order to dwell in a tent or wagon. Don't be so stupid, and stop hanging back or I'll box your ears for you."

Mother Benedicta received her guests with pleasure and no hint of surprise. She had lived too long for random encounters to bother her and she was always grateful to the Holy Spirit when He sent something unusual to stir the convent to life.

As the marquis explained the situation, Mother Benedicta watched Topaz's rapt expression. It wasn't really to be wondered at. Andrew Manners had been an attractive child and now he was a very handsome man. She felt a twinge of compassion for her new fledgling, but it wasn't until some ten minutes later that she realized the marquis had not remained untouched by his encounter with the gypsy girl.

That was a trifle unexpected, but Rossmayne was a man of honour and good sense. It would all be forgotten soon enough. Andrew would go back to the bright lights of the capital and she, Benedicta, would ensure that Topaz was kept too busy to think about things which could break her heart.

"And if you'll undertake her education in addition," said Andrew as he came to the end of his story, "I would be much obliged. I shall provide funds for your Order, naturally. Here is something to go on with; more will be sent within two days."

"You're very generous, my lord." The Mother Superior's lips twitched. "I had never thought of you as a philanthropist."

Andrew didn't smile and for a second his eyes locked with Benedicta's. She felt a small shock as she read the truth, but her expression didn't change.

"No," said the marquis after a second or two. "Perhaps I have been lax in such matters, but that state of affairs can be remedied. Now, my girl, you'll do exactly what Mother Benedicta tells you to do, or any other of the Sisters, come to that. I don't want to hear bad reports about you."

When Topaz had been able to tear her gaze away from Andrew she had looked about her. She felt utterly hemmed in by the panelled walls adorned with religious pictures, crucifixes, statues and ornate candlesticks. She wanted to rush to the door and get out into the open air again before she suffocated.

"I don't want to stay here," she said in a small voice. "Not even to learn to read and write. It feels like a gaol. I have to be free."

"Think yourself lucky it isn't a gaol," returned the marquis tartly. "And don't talk such drivel. You'll get used to it. You can't roam about Dartmoor for the rest of your life."

"No! I must go, I must! I can't breathe."

Rossmayne felt as if he were torturing Topaz, but he had to stand firm. It wasn't only for her sake and the care she would have. Once the heavy doors closed behind him he would never have to see her again.

"Madam, the choice was yours, not mine. If you don't accept sanctuary here, either your family will drag you back, or you'll become a – "

He broke off in deference to the Mother Superior, whose faded grey eyes lit with amusement.

"You may say it, my lord. I'm shock-proof. Those who fight the Devil have to be." She turned to Topaz, taking the small hand in hers and feeling it trembling. "My dear, what the marquis is trying to say is that young women on their own often have to sell their bodies in order to eat."

"I'd never do that." Topaz was indignant, some of her fear dissipating. "I'm not like that."

"You can't be sure. Starvation drives one to extremes."

Topaz had the grace to blush.

"You mean like my borrowing the marquis's horse because I was hungry?"

"Something like that. Ah, here's Sister Mary. She'll look after you. Go with her and she'll shew you the room we keep for visitors. Don't think of it as a cage; it's your home, so learn to love it."

Timothy walked to the door with Sister Mary and Topaz.

"It'll be all right," he said reassuringly. "It's quite remarkable how soon human beings can get used to things."

Topaz looked past him to Rossmayne, still talking to Benedicta.

"Will he come and see me, do you think?"

Amsterdam was wry.

"I wouldn't be at all surprised. He won't want to, but somehow I think he will."

Andrew kissed Mother Benedicta's gnarled hand.

"Thank you. I'm much in your debt."

Once more their eyes met and the old nun said softly:

"I'm sorry, my dear boy, very sorry."

Rossmayne made no attempt to fake a lack of understanding.

"So am I. It was the last thing I expected or wanted to happen."

"God does move in strange ways sometimes, I have to admit. Are things any better between you and Horatia?"

"No, they grow more unbearable with each day that passes."

Rossmayne could be honest with Benedicta. She was the daughter of an earl, well-versed in the ways of the world before she had taken the veil, and he had known her for as long as he could remember.

"I'm sorry about that as well. I shall pray for you."

"And for my little urchin?"

"Especially for her. She loves you, did you know that?"

"I hope you're wrong, for her sake."

"I'm not often wrong, am I?"

"But she's only just met me."

"And you her."

Andrew gave a resigned shrug.

"Yes, you are right, of course. It can happen in a second. I hadn't realized that before. God help her and me, too."

He left the convent with Amsterdam, not turning to look back at the ancient pile. However hopeless things were he was rejoicing because of Benedicta's words which he hugged to himself as if they were precious jewels. He and Topaz had no future, just a brief past, but perhaps he was luckier than most men.

She had brought his heart to life and what she had left in it would never die. He leaned forward to pat Nero's neck and said quietly:

"Come on, Timothy. It's time we went home."

* * *

Andrew and his wife dined alone that night. There weren't many fashionables living on or near Dartmoor and Horatia was constantly complaining about the isolation.

However, the London season was almost upon them and she was more cheerful than she'd been for weeks. Her auburn hair was dressed in the Roman style, her gown an ankle-length shift of green satin covered with net. She was attractive in her own way, growing slightly plump because of her sweet tooth. She was never short of admirers because the invitation in her pale blue eyes drew many men to her.

She had few female friends, for most of her sex saw her as a threat and a shrewish one at that. She had a spiteful twist to her tongue which drove other women away. She didn't care. She had no time for any of them. All she wanted was a doting beau on hand, and Rossmayne's fortune.

She glanced at Andrew, even more silent that evening than usual and gave an exaggerated sigh.

"We shall have to leave for London next week. I must have at least a dozen dresses made before I can shew my face in town. I simply haven't a thing to wear and I won't have people pointing to me as a dowd."

"They're not likely to do that." The marquis's attention was only half-engaged. He was thinking about Topaz's shabby garment which he had torn so roughly. It was probably the only thing she had to put on her back and he had ruined it. "You never seem to appear in the same gown twice running. What on earth do you want with more clothes?"

Horatia's eyes hardened. Sometimes she had to be very firm with Andrew on the question of her lavish expenditure. It was obvious that he didn't care a fig what she looked like, but that was no reason for him to tighten the purse-strings.

"Don't be tiresome, my dear. You don't want our friends to think you keep me short of money, do you?"

"I'm not interested in what they think."

"Well I am." She was growing angry, her voice rising to a pitch which made Rossmayne wince inwardly. "Are you saying I am not to be set up to dine with the Prince at Carlton House? Am I to ride in Hyde Park looking like a washer-woman?"

The marquis gave up. It wasn't worth arguing about. She would pester him until she got exactly what she wanted, down to the last painted fan and embroidered reticule.

"Please yourself. Buy what you like."

"Dear Andrew." Her irritation was over and she was prepared to bestow a smile on him. "I knew you were being thoughtless, rather than mean. I shall go next Tuesday."

"I've no intention of leaving here until May." Rossmayne wasn't sure why it was so important for him to stay on Dartmoor as long as possible, but it was. "You can wait until then, surely?"

The frown was back, her tone shrill again.

"I've just told you why I have to go earlier than that. Really, my lord, you can be most provoking. Do you expect Madame Fleur to make twelve dresses in as many hours? I shall go on ahead with Connell."

Nettie Connell was the marchioness's personal maid and confidante, and Andrew couldn't stand the sight of her. She fawned over Horatia as if the latter were of the blood royal, her shifty brown eyes sliding away from his whenever he looked at her.

"Go then. I don't care what you do."

"How farouche you are. I refuse to stay and talk to you

any longer, and don't come to my room to-night for you will not be welcome."

"I wasn't going to," replied Andrew coolly. "I have better things to do."

"Go to hell, my lord!"

The marquis waited until the door banged shut, shivering on its hinges. Then he leaned back in his chair and started to think of Topaz.

* * *

When Timothy got back to Barrow's End, Lady Agatha was already attired in an elaborate evening gown and a head-band from which a bright blue feather waved precariously. She was fond of her food and liked to dine early.

She was sixty-five years old and confessed to being fifty. Her face was always carefully rouged, her mouth daubed generously with salve. She had out-lived three husbands and gathered in their respective estates, investing the money shrewdly, knowing to a penny what she was worth.

She was tired of London. She had seen all that it had to offer and tasted every one of its delights, many times. When she was ready to retreat to a country life, she chose the place where she had met the only man she had ever loved. He had died before they could marry, but she still dreamed of their long walks on the Moor and the kisses which they had exchanged when they had managed to escape from her chaperone.

"Well, what have you been doing?" she demanded as Timothy bent to kiss her cheek. "You've been out for hours."

"I was with Andrew."

"Poor man. He ought to take a riding-whip to that wife of his and then bed her over and over again until she's with child."

Timothy laughed.

"How very exhausting for him. As to what we've been doing – well – we had something of an adventure to-day."

"Oh?" Agatha thought she caught an odd note in her nephew's voice, but at first a searching glance shewed nothing unusual. "What was the nature of this diversion, may one ask?"

As she listened to Amsterdam she became more sure by the minute that Timothy wasn't quite the same as he'd been when he had left the house that morning. It bothered her, because she adored him. She often urged him to look for a suitable girl, but he always replied that there was plenty of time and to date no one had taken his fancy. Agatha hadn't been unduly concerned. He was young, and marriage was a serious business. Whoever he finally chose would have to come from the right stable.

She turned her head, clicking her fingers impatiently as her maid, Fidelma O'Brien, came into the room.

"Is that my wrap? Great heavens, woman, did you stop to make it? You're getting too fat to hurry yourself up the stairs, that's your trouble."

Fidelma was as unlikely a lady's maid as one could hope to find in a month of Sundays. She was tall, big-boned and well-covered, with grey hair as coarse as a horse's tail straying from her mob-cap. Her face was chubby, her complexion still perfect for all her fifty-eight years, and her green eyes never missed a thing.

"And me with bunions like the fires of hell," she retorted, for she was as close to Lady Agatha as any woman had ever been, and the rapport between them was unique, considering their respective status. "Would you have me get a heart attack just because you haven't the sense to put on a dress fitting for your age?"

"You impertinent besom! I'll have you know this is the very latest design. And another thing. Most ladies' maids try to make something of themselves. You look as if you're about to butcher a carcass."

Fidelma's Irish accent always grew thicker when she was

seized with indignation, and Timothy couldn't always tell what she was talking about, but his aunt knew.

"You want me to flaunt meself before the face of the Holy Virgin in some flimsy shift which leaves no man in doubt as to what's beneath it? That baggage you've just taken on to help in the bedrooms wears one like that and ties her apron right up under her breasts till they nearly pop out, beggin' your pardon, Mr. Timothy. A real whore she looks. I'll stick to my skirts and bodice, thank you very much."

She patted the buffon which concealed her ample bosom, her jaw set ready for a fight.

"What rubbish you do talk. Here, put that thing round my shoulders and then keep your bone-box shut. Mr. Timothy's telling me about a gypsy girl he and Andrew Manners met to-day. Yes, go on, my dear."

"Ah, Mr. Timothy, you don't want to have nothin' to do with them tinkers. All of 'em bad lots. I'd keep clear of 'em if I was you."

"Well you're not him," snapped Agatha and waved her maid aside. "For pity's sake be still and let him get a word in edgeways."

"Mm, I see." Lady Agatha was thoughtful when Amsterdam had finished. She was more bothered than ever, for Timothy's eyes had a dreamy look which she'd never seen in them before, and he'd lingered over the girl's name whenever he had used it. "How old was this wench?"

"Sixteen. She was beautiful. I've never met anyone like her."

"I should hope not." His aunt was severe. "A gypsy child, indeed."

"Doesn't matter what age they are. Right bad lots from the cradle to the grave."

"Fiddy, if you don't hold your tongue I'll send you out of the room."

"Not much point in that. In two seconds you'd be wanting me back for something."

Agatha ignored Fidelma and returned to the much more

worrying matter of Timothy's encounter with a chit called Topaz Chilcott.

"I hope you're not getting absurd ideas about her. The best thing you can do is to forget her."

"I doubt if I'll be able to."

Amsterdam sipped his Madeira, seeing Topaz as clearly as if she were sitting opposite him. He was wondering what it would be like to kiss her when Fidelma repeated her warning.

"Like I says, Mr. Timothy, them tinkers are rotten to the core, to be sure they are."

"She's half-Romany, not a tinker."

"Whatever she is, you'd best leave her be."

"I don't often agree with what this aggravating old fool says, but this time I think she's talking sense."

Amsterdam gave his aunt a lop-sided grin.

"I shan't have any option. Andrew's locked her up in a convent where no one can touch her."

When he went upstairs to change for dinner, Lady Agatha and Fidelma looked at each other.

"I hadn't thought about that," said Agatha pensively. "Why should a man like Rossmayne take such trouble over a gypsy? It's bad enough that Timothy's mooning over her like a schoolboy, wet behind the ears. Surely the marquis hasn't fallen in love with her as well."

"Men are daft enough for anything, you should know that. Saints alive, you've had enough of 'em both sides of the blanket."

"Watch how you speak to me, you cackling hen. Still, you're right. They are a pack of numskulls, the whole boiling of them. Oh well, she's out of their reach now. You know what I think about nuns, but for once they might do something useful."

"Holy women," said Fidelma and bowed her head in respect. "Where should we all be but for their prayers?"

"Exactly where we'd be without them. Pour me some more Madeira and say a prayer yourself."

"What about?"

"That girl, of course, and my nephew. Ask your precious Virgin Mary to give this Romany, or whatever she is, a vocation in the Church, then she'll never bother any of us again. And while she's on the job, she'd better look round for a well-born filly for Timothy to marry. If she doesn't, goodness only knows how all this is going to end. Oh, Fiddy, Fiddy. How very vexing life can be."

* * *

Honor West sat in her bedroom making a painting of the roses which grew just beyond her window.

It was the most precious part of the day to her. From the time she rose in the morning until she mounted the stairs to go to bed, she was at her mother's beck and call. Lady West was domineering, demanding, and critical, Honor being the butt of her discontent and ill-temper.

But between two o'clock and three-thirty, Flora took a nap. Her routine never varied by a second and Honor thought it was probably the spell of freedom after luncheon which enabled her to remain sane.

When she went down to the sitting-room to pour tea for her mother, the latter was in one of her most waspish moods.

"Been wasting your time drawing again, I suppose. I can't think why you bother, for you've no talent. Why don't you do something useful like sewing? I could do with several new shifts and caps and you know we haven't enough money to keep calling in the seamstress."

Honor didn't reply, passing her mother's cup to her.

"Well, answer me. Don't sit there sulking. It's no good pretending you've any aptitude for art when it's quite clear you've none at all. I suppose you were dreaming about Timothy Amsterdam again. Really, Honor, you are so stupid."

Honor looked up at Lady West, a large woman with

white hair puffed out round her lawn cap, and a heavy nose over thin, disgruntled lips. Flora had never forgiven her husband for dying ten years before, leaving her badly off. She had had to cut the number of servants employed and practice many other economies, none of which affected her personally. As soon as Honor was old enough she had been dragooned into helping with the housework, preparing meals if cook were ill, as well as acting as her mother's companion.

Honor had loved Timothy since she was eight years old. She didn't really know what it was about him which made her go pale whenever they met and kept her awake at night longing for him. She could see that he wasn't good-looking like Andrew Manners, but each line of his face was dear to her. He was so kind and good, and Honor felt as though she were being blessed whenever he spoke to her.

The trouble was that Timothy didn't return her feelings. Indeed, she was sure he hardly realized she was alive, save that they had known each other for a long time. She was just someone vaguely in the background of his life to whom he was courtesy itself when they did encounter each other.

"Well?"

Lady West wasn't going to let the subject drop and Honor sighed.

"I'm not good with my needle, mother. I can't help it."

"You're no good with a paintbrush either, but you still waste time wielding one. And don't tell me you weren't thinking of Amsterdam, because I shan't believe you."

"Does it hurt to think about a friend once in a while?"

"Pass me a scone and don't use that tone of voice with me. It's more than just thinking about him, isn't it? You're sick with love for him, but he'd never give a plain Jane like you a second's thought."

"Yet if I could make him notice me perhaps he might consider my suitability as a wife. As we're so poor, it would be an advantage if I could marry someone with money."

"It certainly would. No one would be more grateful than I if I could stop looking at every penny, but you won't catch

Amsterdam, so you might as well stop trying. What about Mr. Chambers? He's more likely to suit as I've told you before."

Honor wanted to scream. Mr. Chambers' name and virtues had been the main topic of her mother's conversation for the last two months, and no matter how many times Honor expressed her dislike of the man, Flora continued to press the subject.

"But he's a tradesman."

Lady West snorted.

"What of it? Not what I would have chosen, of course, but he's got plenty of money, isn't that so, Tipper?"

Ida Tipper had just slipped into the room with more hot water. She was middle-aged, thin as a bean-pole, with small eyes and a mouth puckered up with spite.

"Mother!"

"Don't be so absurd. Tipper knows our situation. She's my personal maid, not like the other servants."

"Thank you, m'lady." Tipper preened. She was detested below stairs because she was forever carrying tales concerning the short-comings of the rest of the staff. "If you were speaking of Mr. George Chambers, you're quite right. As they say in the North, he's a warm man. Good solid business and still expanding."

"But he's old, mother."

"Don't be ridiculous. He can't be more than fifty."

"That is old – oh! I didn't mean that you –"

"Such tact." Flora was scathing. "What an asset you'd be entertaining Amsterdam's guests. I'm not old and neither is Chambers. He'd like to marry into our circle, for he's a snob."

"You're right again, m'lady." Tipper nodded, making things as bad for Honor as she could. The girl had a way of looking at her as if she could read her mind and Ida didn't like it. "Miss Honor would suit him well. Give him a bit of tone, as it were. Reckon he'd be generous if he got a chance like that."

"Yes, I shall have to think about it." Flora took a large bite out of her third scone. "Difficult to invite a tradesman to one's house, but the bills are piling up so quickly I may have no choice."

"You may invite him a hundred times," said Honor tightly, "but I will never marry him."

"You'll do what I tell you."

"No, I won't."

"What an awkward, obstinate creature you are. No sense of gratitude for all I've done for you, utterly graceless, and an extra mouth to feed."

"I do my full share of the work in this house and I wait on you. I don't eat much, but what I do I earn. Now, if you'll excuse me –"

"Don't go running off for long. I want you to write some letters. Just wash your hands and then come back. You've frittered away enough time for one day."

In her bedroom, Honor gazed at herself in the cracked mirror, a sense of hopelessness bringing tears to her eyes. Her reflection shewed exactly what she imagined Timothy must see when he looked at her. A round face, too plump in the cheeks, a retroussé nose, and eyes neither blue nor grey but somewhere indeterminately in between. Her hair was brown and, to her, quite impossibly dull and lifeless. Her mother was right; Timothy wouldn't want a woman as plain as she.

She was quite unconscious of the sweet, wholesome appearance she presented. Her lips were full and generous, the eyes, if not the fashionable bright blue, were clear and honest. There were red lights in her curls which she had never noticed and her complexion was without flaw.

She turned away from the looking-glass, pouring water into the china bowl by her bed.

"If I can't have you," she said aloud, for she often conversed with Timothy in that one-sided manner, "then I won't have anyone. I'd rather stay with mother and become a real old maid. As for George Chambers, I'd prefer to go on the streets than become his.

"Oh, Timothy, dear Timothy! Why can't you see how much I love you?"

* * *

Topaz soon set the Convent of St. Francis on its ear. Most of the Sisters were shocked to the core by her blunt speech and colourful curses.

She had announced at once that she didn't believe in God. The nuns had gasped and gone to the Mother Superior for reassurance that they wouldn't be infected by the infidel in their midst.

"She denies Our Lord, Mother," said Sister Martha in alarm. "And she says there is no point in praying to someone who doesn't exist."

"She is not suited to such a place as this." Sister Cecilia was flushed with vexation. "This morning I caught her in my cell. I explained to her that our enclosures are very special to us, but she didn't seem to understand. She just said my prayer-desk would be useful to climb on to look out of the window."

"And the other day she asked me if Sister Matthew John was a man." Sister Agnes was scandalised. "I can speak of it now, since our dear companion is in the infirmary. I asked the child why she should imagine such a thing. She said that Sister Matthew John had a man's name and a moustache."

"She has such an odd name. She should be called after one of the saints."

"And those earrings! Gold hoops which rattle when she runs, and she's always running somewhere. They should be taken away from her, for it is nothing short of blasphemy for her to flaunt them as she does."

Mother Benedicta, immaculate in her black habit and white, starched coif, listened to her flock, her eyes twinkling.

"I don't think I'd go that far, Sister Margaret. When I

was young I had earrings shaped like hoops, too. They were made of diamonds, not gold, but I wore them when I went to a ball and never felt my immortal soul in danger because of that.

"You must be patient with Topaz. Remember, all her life she has wandered from place to place, sleeping in a tent or under the stars. She finds our convent hateful because it cuts her off from the light, the air, and the sun to which she is accustomed. And what if she does run instead of walking? Didn't we all do so at her age? She can't be expected to appreciate what our cells mean to us. To her, they are simply rooms, and her dead mother chose her name. As to Sister Matthew John – "

Benedicta was trying hard to keep a straight face. She had more than once been guilty of the unkind opinion that the gaunt, ageing nun had a somewhat masculine cast of countenance. She had confessed her sin and done her penance, but then she would encounter Sister Matthew John again and the same unworthy thought would pop back into her head once more.

"Now, my dears." Her voice became firmer. "I realize how alien Topaz's behaviour must seem to you, but God has sent her to us to teach and train and to make her accept Him, as we do. It won't be easy, but worthwhile things seldom are. Try to ignore the things which aren't really important and concentrate upon those which matter."

The Sisters went off unconvinced, but a month later some had softened slightly towards their wayward guest. It hadn't taken Sister Anne long to discover how intelligent Topaz was and, as the former was a born teacher, she forgot all about the gold earrings and the unseemly deportment and got down to business.

Topaz was no happier at the convent after four weeks incarcerated within its walls, but she was growing used to many things. She loved her lessons, always asking questions, swift to learn, greedy for more information.

The refectory where meals were served was still a bit

daunting. It was a large room, totally silent save for the voice of one Sister perched up on a pulpit in the end wall, reading portions of the scriptures. Every day Topaz watched to see if the Sister would fall off her perch, but she never did.

The nuns sat with their backs to the walls without uttering a word. At first, Topaz thought they must have quarrelled but, as the stillness was never broken, she concluded it was yet another odd custom practised by the strange women who surrounded her.

Although she had rejected the Almighty, Mother Benedicta had asked her to attend Mass. She had been shewn into a side chapel set apart for visitors. Peering through the wrought iron barrier she watched the nuns file into their stalls, wondering why there was a screen separating what she had been told was the sanctuary from the rest of the chapel. It seemed that wherever a wall or something similar could be built, one had appeared. Yet none of the inmates looked worried about the prison they had embraced.

After a while she began to enjoy the pure clear voices of the Sisters. She thought they must like singing very much since they went to the chapel so often. It was Sister Anne who explained the never-ending cycle of prayer; Matins, Lauds, Prime, Terce, Sext, None, Vespers and Compline.

"Don't you ever get tired?" she asked Sister Anne as the latter opened her book ready for that day's study. "You get up so early and when you're not in chapel, you're scrubbing or polishing or digging in the garden."

Sister Anne was young and ardent and she understood Topaz better than most of her companions.

"Of course we do, but our devotions bring us nothing but joy and work never hurt anyone. Didn't you have to work when you were with your family?"

"Yes, all the time, but that was different."

"Why?"

"Well – " Topaz stopped and shook her head. "I don't know. It just wasn't the same. I helped with the animals, collected firewood and looked after those who died. Romanies won't touch the dead if they can possibly help it. Some pay the *gaujos* to lay out the body, but in our tribe it was my job."

Sister Anne was shaken.

"You laid out the dead?"

"Yes, always. I washed them, then dressed them in their best clothes, but never new ones. They had to be garments they'd worn at least once before. I'd put money in their pockets and their favourite possessions by their side and then the others would wait by the death-tent until it was time to bury 'em."

"Good gracious! How long had you been doing that?"

"Since I was nine."

"How – how painful for you."

"I didn't mind much; I got used to it. The others in the family didn't like me because I wasn't of pure blood. That's why I got all the dirty work to do. I'm not liked in the convent either, am I?"

"My dear, of course you are. We love you because you were sent to us by Our Father."

"He must have been splitting His sides when He put the idea into the marquis's head to leave me here. Not that I believe in this God of yours, you understand."

"You will one day. I have utmost faith in that and I'm very fond of you."

Even mentioning the marquis's name made the dull ache inside Topaz worse. Despite all the new experiences she was going through, the thought of Rossmayne never left her. When she was lying on her thin pallet at night she screwed her eyes up tight and then she could see his face. Sometimes he was angry as he'd been when they had fought. At other times the lines of his mouth were softer and she longed to lay her lips against his.

She saw her tutor's enquiring look and dismissed her benefactor for the moment. She gave Sister Anne a smile and the young nun thought she had never seen such absolute perfection of countenance in another human being.

"I like you, too," said Topaz reassuringly. "I don't think Mother Benedicta hates me, but I'm sure Sister Matthew John and Sister Margaret do. Sister Margaret is always nagging me about my earrings and telling me to take them off, but I'm not going to. They were my mother's and the only things I have of hers."

"Then keep them on. Sister Margaret will get used to them in time. Perhaps you could meet her half-way and not rattle them so much during Mass."

Topaz chuckled.

"All right, I'll try to remember. Do you think I'll soon learn to read and write?"

"Not if we keep gossiping like this."

"I'd like to write to the marquis and thank him for what he did for me. Do you think he'll visit us soon?"

Sister Anne was wary. It wasn't the first time her pupil had mentioned Rossmayne and each time the girl's face had lit up in a way which made the nun catch her breath. Anne wasn't worried about any sin involved; she just didn't want Topaz to be hurt.

"I doubt it. He's done his duty so there's nothing to bring him back."

Topaz sighed.

"No, I suppose not. If I did believe in God, I'd pray to Him to get the marquis to come."

"Such entreaty wouldn't be answered if what you sought was likely to bring you pain."

"But it wouldn't, truly it wouldn't."

"Not truly, Topaz. Don't use that word so lightly. The reason you want to see his lordship has nothing to do with gratitude and you know it. Be sensible, my dear, and put him out of your mind."

"I don't think I'll ever be able to do that."

"You must try harder. There's nothing but sorrow for you along that road."

"I suppose so. Still – "

"Now that's enough talk for to-day. Open your book at page four – yes – just there. I'll read a sentence, then you repeat it."

"Would you like me to accept God?"

"Naturally I would."

"Perhaps I'll think about it, for your sake."

"Not for my sake. You mustn't do anything especially for me. That would be very wrong. You have to love each of us equally and worship God for His sake, not because it would please me."

Topaz gave an even deeper sigh.

"I've got a lot to learn, haven't I?"

"Indeed you have, but I'm here to give you instruction. That is, if you'll stop talking long enough for me to do my job."

"Just one more question."

"The very last, mind."

"I promise. In the end, will I be worth something if I pay great attention to all that you tell me?"

Anne smiled.

"You're worth a great deal now, but yes. I can't see into the future in the way you said your Aunt Liti could do, but I'm certain of this, for I feel it in my bones.

"One day, this Order is going to be very proud of you, Topaz Chilcott; very proud indeed."

Three

On the last day of October, Horatia Rossmayne disappeared. She left Grimspound where High Brook, the marquis's country seat, lay in a shallow valley between Hameldon Tor and Hockney Tor.

The Rossmaynes had lived there since the sixteenth century, the house stubbornly resisting the elements which tried to erode its walls. There was little to be seen around it. Just stretches of heather and whortleberry, with a few stunted trees here and there to break the skyline.

The marchioness had set out early, announcing she was going to visit friends near Yellowmead Down. Intransigent as always, she had refused to allow either her maid or a groom to accompany her.

"I'm not going to John O'Groats," she'd said as she had cantered off. "Stop fussing, all of you. I'll be back by three."

The fog came down after luncheon. It rolled towards High Brook in thin, vaporous strands, giving the house a spectral aspect. Soon it thickened to a grey blanket, wrapping itself round the windows so that every candle in the place had to be lit.

The servants watched the clock in the kitchen tick away the minutes. They didn't like their mistress, but they were sorry for anyone out on the Moor on a day like that.

Denning, the butler, was worried. The marquis and Amsterdam had gone to Plymouth the day before, intending to stay the night. He wasn't sure what to do about the missing woman, wondering where on earth she could be, until a knock at the rear entrance answered the question for him.

Andrew and Timothy got home at nine. By then the mist had lifted and sharp needles of rain had driven into them relentlessly.

"Thank heavens that's over." The marquis handed his greatcoat to Denning. "We're starving. I hope the dinner isn't burnt. Is her ladyship upstairs?"

It was then that he noticed the two men standing behind the butler in the shadows. They had weather-beaten faces, smocks which could withstand rain and snow and wore highlows which made muddy marks on the floor where they shuffled their feet. Their billycock hats were in their hands, twisted out of shape by nervous fingers, and neither man looked up to meet the marquis's eyes.

"Well, who have we here, Denning?"

The butler swallowed hard.

"This is Sam Butterworth, my lord, and this Jack Clibber. They're shepherds from Cawley Farm."

The marquis's brows rose. Shepherds and their kind didn't normally wait in the main hall of High Brook.

"A pleasure, gentlemen, but why are you here – at this time of night?"

The moormen exchanged an uneasy glance, but it was left to Denning to state the purpose of their visit.

"They have news of her ladyship, sir."

Andrew felt a sudden twinge of apprehension.

"Oh?"

"Yes, m'lord." Denning hurried on. "Her ladyship went to see the Wentworths. She wouldn't take a groom with her although I warned her that the fog might come down later."

The marquis turned back to the moormen.

"I see. She went out early this morning and hasn't returned. And you have news of her? Speak plainly if you please. Where is my wife now?"

"It be difficult to know how to say it, sir." Butterworth had pushed Clibber forward to be spokesman. "Aye, very difficult."

"For God's sake stop shilly-shallying. Where is she?"

"In Foxton Mire, m'lord."

Andrew was aware that Amsterdam had said something under his breath, but for a moment he was transfixed. Many times he had wished Horatia to perdition, particularly since he had met Topaz, but he had never meant her real harm.

"Foxton Mire?" His voice sounded odd to him, as if someone were speaking for him. "But that's nowhere near the direct track from Yellowmead Down to Grimspound."

"Reckon she lost her way." Clibber was still looking down at his feet. "But that's where she were right enough. We saw and 'eard her."

The marquis was very calm.

"You'd better tell me all about it. When did you see her?"

"Three hours since. Me and Sam missed our way and found ourselves on the edge of Foxton Mire. It were 'ard to see, but we could 'ear someone screamin'. We walked a bit nearer, careful like, and then the mist rolled away for a minute or two and there she was. Up to 'er shoulders by then, shrieking like a banshee. We yelled to 'er to keep still while we looked round for summat to throw to 'er to catch 'old of. Don't think she 'eard, for she were still cryin' out fit to deafen us, beggin' your pardon, m'lord."

Andrew waved a hand. He didn't really need to hear the rest, although he had to brace himself to listen. The end of the moorman's tale was all too predictable.

"We couldn't find nothin'," said Butterworth, speaking for the first time, bolder now that the truth was out. "We went back to the edge of the mire, but she'd gorn."

"Did you see her horse?"

"Nary a trace of him."

"My dear Andrew." Timothy wasn't sure what to say. "This is dreadful."

"Yes, it is. Butterworth, Clibber, it's not that I doubt you, but I want to see for myself. It's just possible that when the two of you were hunting for a means of rescuing the marchioness she could have pulled herself out and reached firm ground."

"Nay, sir. She were sucked under right enough."

"Nevertheless, I must be sure. I cannot ignore even the slightest chance that she may have survived. I want you to come with me. You can shew me the exact spot and that will save time. I'll pay you well. You would know where to find the place, I suppose?"

At that moment Timothy glanced at the two shepherds who had drawn back in consternation. He had never seen fear more clearly written on human faces and for a brief second he was puzzled. Then he dismissed his doubts. Men like Butterworth and Clibber were born and bred in an atmosphere of superstition and folk-lore.

"You don't have to be afraid," he said, trying to allay their terror. "There are no demons in the Mire. That's only an old wives' tale. And the marquis and I will be there. You must help us. We could spend the rest of the night looking if we have no guides."

In the end, Butterworth and Clibber gave their reluctant assent. Their cheeks were blanched and drawn as the party set out in the driving rain, armed with ropes and fresh lanterns.

When they reached the area where the shepherds had seen Horatia, Timothy felt as if a clammy hand had reached out and touched his spine. The place had a bad name and was avoided by locals, even when the sun was shining. In the darkness and wet it lived up to its evil reputation. It smelt of death and decay, lying green and treacherous like a contented animal which had just been fed, but one which was also ready for a second helping.

Having skirted the mire itself without success, the search-party fanned out to cover a wider area, calling Horatia's name. It was useless. No one was near Foxton Mire that night except themselves.

"I told 'ee, m'lord," said Butterworth, wiping the moisture from his face. "She went under. No livin' soul could 'ave pulled 'emselves out o' that bog. Up to 'er shoulders, she were. Then it would 'ave been 'er neck and then – "

"For Christ's sake!" Timothy was violent. "We don't need pictures drawn for us. Watch what you're saying."

Butterworth mumbled an apology, still looking scared to death.

"Here's your money." The marquis threw the shepherd a purse. "I'm grateful to you for your help and for coming to High Brook in the first place. I regret dragging you back here, but I had to be certain."

The moormen pocketed their reward and trudged off, but Andrew didn't move.

"We should go," said Amsterdam after a moment. "You're soaked."

"No more than you are, but you're right. There's nothing we can do here. It seems worse because I didn't love her. I ought to feel something for her now that she's gone, but I don't."

"It'll be different in the morning."

"I doubt it. I must send a letter to her parents first thing to-morrow and then make arrangements for the funeral. How odd it will be. We shall be burying an empty coffin."

"Don't think about it now."

"It's difficult not to, isn't it? I didn't have a lot of affection for her, but I wouldn't wish such a fate on my worst enemy.

"Dear God, Timothy. It was a terrible way to die."

* * *

A year later, when autumn came again to the Moor, Topaz Chilcott climbed her favourite slope and sank down to enjoy the copper and bronze glory of the dying year. The wind blew her hair out behind her as she held up her face to the sun, still warm in its caress.

It hadn't taken Benedicta long to realize that it would be sheer cruelty to keep the marquis's protegée penned within the confines of the convent. She needed some freedom if she were ever going to settle, never mind blossom.

A promise was extracted from Topaz that she would never go too far or stay away too long. The vow was readily given and from that day the alteration in her life began.

She proved a quick, intelligent scholar, the pride of Sister Anne's heart, but there was more to her slow metamorphosis than mere book learning. She made strenuous efforts to tame her behaviour when she was indoors, never rattling her earrings during Mass, nor racing along the stone corridors as if they were open fields. Now and then there was an outburst of rebellion but, as the months passed, these grew fewer and fewer.

She was more captivating than ever. Good food, plenty of

sleep, and the knowledge that she was really wanted and loved gave her face a serenity it had never had before.

Latterly, she had stopped saying that she didn't believe in God. It wasn't just to please her companions, but because she was beginning to have doubts about her original opinion. The Mother Superior noted this at once, but was far too wise to press Topaz, and warned the other Sisters not to do so either. She simply answered any questions Topaz raised and left the rest to the Holy Spirit.

Topaz's only sorrow was that she hadn't seen the marquis again. She thought about him constantly, longing for a sight of him. A girl who came from the village to help with the laundry had told the Community of the marchioness's death. Topaz had shuddered at the horror of it, but couldn't help weaving a future in which Andrew sought her out, courted her, and finally offered for her hand. It was pure fantasy and she knew it. The marquis would have to marry a woman of noble blood, but that didn't stop Topaz from wanting and loving him.

She had to accept the fact that he might not return to the convent and, sad though it made her, she would often lay her cheek against the rough heather and whisper his name. It seemed to tighten the tenuous link between them, even as she wept for him.

"I expect he's forgotten me, don't you?" Topaz talked to the Moor as if it were a friend, and on that particular day she wanted to share her thoughts with the vastness around her. "Perhaps I'll never see him again. It's such a pity because I do adore him so."

The wind swirled round her harder than before, as if in answer. She laughed.

"Yes, I hear you, and I'm a ninny, but don't tease me because I'm really very unhappy about it all."

Benedicta was in the hall when Topaz got back. She gazed at the girl's wild-rose cheeks and half-closed eyes.

"You're day-dreaming again," she said. "Was it a happy dream?"

Topaz was brought up short. She was always forgetting how perceptive Mother Benedicta was.

"Not really," she replied awkwardly. "It wasn't anything special. I've forgotten it already."

"I hope you have. That sort of dream can only do you harm."

She nodded as Topaz curtsied and then made her stately way to where Sister Agnes was sewing drawers for her Sisters in God.

"Topaz needs a new gown," said the Mother Superior. "The one she's wearing now is getting very tight across the – well – it's getting tight in the wrong places. Have we any suitable material? I'd like her to have something other than fustian."

"We've got that flowered percale sent as a gift, Mother." Agnes was a comfortable bundle of a woman with innocence in her eyes and magic in her hands. "We didn't know what to do with it at the time, if you remember."

"Ah yes, well we know how to use it now. Take some measurements and be generous with your inches. Our foundling is fast becoming a woman. We can't give her what she really wants, poor girl, but at least we can make her look pretty. Flowered percale isn't much of a substitute for love, but that's all we can offer."

Sister Agnes looked blank and Benedicta laughed.

"Take no notice of me. It's one of my silly days. I find they're becoming more frequent with age. Just get busy with your needle and see if the work can be done by Friday. Yes, Friday would be very nice. Bless you, my dear. What should we all do without your nimble fingers?"

* * *

Two days later, Andrew Manners went riding alone in the direction of Wild Tor.

He had wanted to go to the convent many times, but common sense and will-power had won the day until then.

After Horatia's funeral he had gone to London, spending a year in a frenzy of gambling, drinking, fast riding and the seduction of women. None of these activities had blotted out the picture of what Horatia's last moments must have been like. Even less had they diminished the image of Topaz which was always in his mind's eye.

The greater the longing he felt for her the more sensible he had tried to be. He needed an heir, and was about to make a formal offer for the hand of Virginia Grafton. Lord and Lady Grafton were well-pleased with the impending engagement. Rossmayne's lineage was impeccable, his fortune large. They had brushed aside criticisms of Andrew's recent behaviour. What man wouldn't go half off his head in such circumstances? Once married to their daughter, they averred, he would settle down and any scandal would soon be forgotten.

They had been careful not to let Rossmayne know just how delicate Virginia's constitution was. Their doctor had murmured something about a weak heart, but Lord Grafton had dismissed the warning, saying the physician was an old woman. Lady Grafton had agreed readily with her spouse. She wanted her daughter to be a marchioness, maintaining that there was nothing wrong with Virginia which marriage wouldn't cure.

As he rode on, Andrew thought briefly and dispassionately about his bride-to-be. She was a blue-eyed blonde, possessed of graceful manners, and would be an amenable wife. He didn't love her, and never would but, as Timothy had once said, few men married for that reason.

When he saw Topaz climbing down a rough slope he brought Nero to a halt, an overwhelming surge of life running through him as if he were being born anew.

Her hair was the plaything of the rough breeze as she ran towards him and he caught his breath. She was exquisite, even in a shabby dark gown, and as she came up to him he saw the luminous eyes filled with what he most wanted to see.

Topaz was slightly out of breath as she reached the marquis, not quite able to believe he was really there. She had dreamed of such a moment so often. Now it had come and for once she was tongue-tied.

Andrew dismounted, trying to ignore the fact that her body was maturing in a way which made his blood race, and that she was almost ripe for love-making. He was a free man now, but Topaz could never become his wife. He could look at her, yearn for her, but never touch her because he had no right to the adoration he saw in her eyes.

Mother Benedicta had told him that Topaz loved him. If he had had any doubts about that her expression dispelled them. They both loved deeply, but all they would ever be able to talk about were small, unimportant things.

"Well?" he asked lightly. "And how is my little horse-thief?"

Topaz knew that he was teasing her and her first nervousness was gone.

"A reformed character, my lord."

"That I doubt. Have you learned to read and write yet?"

"Yes and I know quite a bit about history, geography and Latin. Sister Anne is teaching me French and she says my accent is really very good."

"Remarkable." He was still derisive, knowing that he dared not become serious with her. "At least my money hasn't been wasted."

"No it hasn't and I do thank you for your help. Something quite marvellous has happened. Shall I tell you about it? We could sit on that stone over there if you liked."

Topaz found herself praying to a God in whom she didn't quite believe that Andrew would agree and stay with her for a while. He probably wouldn't be very interested in what she had to say, but at least he would be near her and she could dwell upon the handsome face which was exactly as she had remembered it.

The marquis nodded, feigning indifference.

"As you wish. What is this world-shaking announcement

you have to make?"

"Mother Benedicta told me yesterday that in a year or two I'm to go to the village of Yelton. The Order has a place there. It's only a barn, really, but the Sisters do much good amongst the poor and sick. I've been working in our infirmary for quite a while now, that is, when I'm not having my ordinary lessons. Mother says I have a true feeling for medicine."

Andrew fell silent. Yelton was even nearer to Grimspound than High Tor. The temptation to see Topaz would increase. It was just as well that he would soon be yoked to Virginia, so that his desire for his headstrong gypsy would never be allowed free rein.

"Aren't you pleased? I thought you would. At least I shall be doing something useful."

He threw off his worry and said quickly:

"Of course I am, if that will give you what you want from life."

He saw her change from a carefree girl into a woman in the space of two seconds, the eyes which met his filled with pain.

"What I want from life I cannot have. This is the best I can manage."

He knew what she meant and stepped back quickly from such dangerous ground.

"I must be careful not to get sick or become poor."

She was laughing again, her true self hidden from him.

"I'd treat you well, my lord. I would feed you with hot gruel. I'm rather good at making that."

"The very thought of it chills me to the bone."

There was a brief pause. Then Topaz said hopefully:

"Will you be riding this way again?"

He meant to give her an emphatic no, but the word was never uttered. London in three days' time and Virginia. Then a last few weeks of freedom at High Brook. He and Topaz would only meet and talk, and that wasn't asking much from spiteful Fate. There would be so many empty years when finally they had to say good-bye.

"I may do, when I return from town. I make no promises."

"Of course not. I'll be here every morning in case you decide to come."

What he heard in her voice made him frown and try to warn her.

"Topaz – "

"Yes?"

When it came to it he couldn't kill the happiness he saw in her. The curve of her red mouth and the wash of colour in her cheeks bemused him. She filled him with a kind of exultation he had never experienced before and he found himself shaking his head.

"It's nothing. Go back to your books and behave yourself."

"I would work much harder if you came now and then so that I could tell you of my progress."

He gave a faint laugh.

"You're still a hussy, Topaz Chilcott. Be off with you."

"Before I go I want to thank you."

"You've done so already."

"Yes, but I want to do it properly."

"How many ways are there to express gratitude? In any case, you owe me nothing."

"I owe you everything and here is my 'thank you'."

He felt her lips against his, soft, warm, sensuous. Then she was flying off as if caught up by the wind. He waited until she was out of sight before raising his hand to where her mouth had rested. Half-child, half-woman, she was wholly female. If he could have pulled her into his arms at that moment he knew nothing could have stopped him from making love to her.

"Rossmayne," he said under his breath. "You are a damned fool."

And leaping into the saddle he raced back to

Grimspound, Nero at full stretch, the Devil laughing and snapping at his heels as he went.

* * *

The ball to celebrate the betrothal of the marquis and Virginia Grafton started well enough.

Everybody who was anybody had gathered in Lord Grafton's spacious house in Grosvenor Square. There was music and dancing, rich fare, a river of wine, and the whole of society shewing off its most exotic garb.

Virginia stood beside Andrew shivering, despite the heat of the room. Everyone said how lucky she was to have snared such a prize as the marquis, but she would have given anything to have changed places with Mary Waters, her maid, who was fat, plain and single. She couldn't imagine what it would be like having to get into bed with the elegant stranger who turned to speak to her now and then. From what her mother had told her the experience would be horrendous and she had cried herself to sleep for the past week thinking about it.

It was after supper that Virginia collapsed as she was dancing with Andrew. He carried her to a side room, Lady Grafton, resplendent in draped red silk and turban headdress, hurrying beside him, thoroughly irritated with her daughter for shewing such weakness.

"We should get a doctor," said Rossmayne when he had laid Virginia on a couch. "We must find out what's wrong with her."

Lady Grafton's laugh was high and artificial.

"My dear Andrew, don't fuss. She's only fainted. It's all the excitement."

"But she's so pale."

"That will pass. It does get warm in the ball-room, especially when there are so many present. Look, she's coming round. I'll send for some brandy and then she'll be her old self again."

Brandy arrived and with it came Mary, carrying a wrap, aromatic salts and a fan, ready for any eventuality.

"It won't hurt the child to rest for a while," said Lady Grafton archly. "I'm sure you and she have much to talk about, my lord. Take no notice of Waters. She's right at the other end of the room and is deaf and blind when she has to be."

Andrew wasn't sorry to see his future mother-in-law depart. She was somewhat dictatorial and he hadn't liked the total lack of sympathy she had shewn for her daughter.

"I'm sorry." Virginia was stricken. She had disgraced herself in public, which was bad enough. But that wasn't all. There was every likelihood now that the marquis would try to withdraw from the match. No man wanted a wife who kept having the vapours. A release from the betrothal would be more than welcome, but her mother would exact a terrible price if such a disaster occurred. "It was very foolish of me."

Andrew looked at her meditatively. Since he had decided to make Virginia his spouse he had seen her fairly frequently. It was true that she was slight and delicate looking, but that was fashionable. She had always had pink in her cheeks and soft rose on her lips. Now he was beginning to wonder if the colour had been natural. She had been as light as a feather to carry and her small hands were as cold as ice. He hadn't noticed before just how thin she was, and that night it was obvious that her maid had been over-generous with the rouge-brush.

"You couldn't help it."

"But I'm so ashamed."

"For heaven's sake why?" He was quick to comfort her, for her blue eyes had filled with tears. "There's nothing to be ashamed about. As your mother said, it was the excitement of the occasion."

"I'll try never to do it again."

He realized that she was pleading for some reason, but wasn't quite sure why.

"Stop worrying. Women do faint now and then. It isn't a crime."

"No, but I did want to be a good wife to you and mother said men didn't like weaklings. If I keep doing this you won't want me."

"You'll be a most excellent wife and I shall fatten you up so that you never swoon again. You look as if you need a good meal. Have you had anything to eat to-night?"

"No, I wasn't hungry."

"Then it's not surprising that you felt unwell." He raised his voice. "Mary, go and fetch your mistress some cold chicken and fruit, will you? Oh, and some wine, too, please."

When the maid had gone he looked back at Virginia's woe-begone face, aware of something else which he hadn't seen before.

"Virginia, you're not afraid of me, are you?"

She went red with mortification.

"I try not to be, sir, but I've never met anyone like you before. The other men who have called on me seemed so young. Oh, I don't mean that you're old. How dreadful of me to imply such a thing."

"I'm twenty-five," he said dryly. "The grave seems a long way off."

"I keep saying the wrong things. You must think me very gauche."

He studied her downcast lashes and said softly:

"That's not what makes you fear me, is it?"

Her admission was slow to come.

"No, my lord. I don't know how to say this because I'm so embarrassed."

"Try. It takes a lot to disconcert me."

She braced herself as if she were going into battle, blurting the truth out as she clasped her hands together until the knuckles stood out like bleached bones.

"Well, mother explained to me what was expected of me in the marriage bed and it sounded so terrifying. I'm not sure that I can – well – that I'd be able to – "

"I see." The marquis was furious with Lady Grafton for her insensibility which bordered on cruelty. "No wonder you're frightened out of your wits. Ignore her and listen to me. I'm not going to rape you. I'll teach you what pleasure there is in making love and I'll give you all the time you need to adjust to your new circumstances."

"You're very kind," she said shyly. "I hadn't expected that."

"No, after your mother's tuition I don't suppose you did." He was still angry. "I suspect that kindness doesn't play much part in your life."

"I thought you might want to break off the match after I'd made an exhibition of myself."

"Break off the match because of so small a thing? What a goose you are."

Andrew watched Virginia peck daintily at her food, remembering how Topaz had tucked in with gusto at the inn where he and Timothy had taken her.

He couldn't imagine Topaz fainting. Slender though she was, she had real stamina. She was like Mother Earth, born to bear sons.

But Virginia could do that, too. He dismissed any previous misgivings because all at once he felt protective towards the girl on the couch. Removed from her abominable parent, and cared for properly, she would give him the heir he needed. She was looking better already and he nodded in satisfaction.

"I want you to promise to eat well in the future," he said, "and look after yourself. I want a plump wife and a happy one, otherwise we shall never get ourselves a family."

She was overcome by confusion at his bluntness. However, the marquis was looking at her with affection and she took courage in both hands.

"I'll have lots of babies, sir. As many as you want, that is, if you will help me."

At first, she was utterly bewildered when he burst out

laughing. Then she realized what she had said and put a hand over her mouth in consternation.

"Oh, my lord." She began to laugh with him. "Aren't I too ridiculous for words?"

"You are delightful," he replied, and pushed the vision of Topaz out of his mind, for she had no place there now. "And call me Andrew; it is my name, you know. I think we are going to deal very well together, don't you?"

"I hope so." Her wide eyes were on his. "I want to please you and you're not a bit as I expected you to be."

"Then a kiss to seal the bargain."

Her lips had no magic in them and he felt nothing but pity for her. She would have his name and all that was his, but his love belonged to Topaz and always would.

"Now it is my turn to be sorry," he said, knowing she wouldn't understand what he meant. "Forgive me, my dear."

As he had expected, she assumed his apology was because he had been so bold in the maid's presence.

"Don't worry," she said comfortingly. "Mary wasn't looking and I found the experience very pleasant. It's the first time it's ever happened to me, you see, and I'm not in the least afraid any more."

"I'm glad."

Her innocent pleasure made her seem even more vulnerable and he sighed inwardly. Small things would make her happy; one harsh word would send her into the depths of despair. He would have to be very careful how he handled his bride, for she had been injured enough.

"Andrew, did you hear what I said?"

He came out of his reverie to find her smiling at him.

"I'm sorry, Virginia, I was miles away. What did you say?"

She blushed charmingly and laid a hand over his.

"I think I would like you to kiss me again. Indeed, I am sure I would because I believe I'm falling in love with you. Now, isn't that the nicest thing for both of us?"

Four

When Andrew returned to Dartmoor he rode out to High Tor to look for Topaz.

Prior to his departure for London they had seen each other once or twice. He hadn't said a great deal, content to look at her as she told him all about life in the convent and of the strange foibles of some of her companions.

He had no idea what an effort it had been for Topaz to keep up the easy flow of chatter. She had been tortured by his closeness, knowing she couldn't so much as touch his hand. But she loved him enough to understand his silence and found courage from somewhere for both of them.

The winter was particularly venomous that year. The rain fell almost horizontally, its bite as sharp as darts. The wind was violent and felt substantial enough to lean against. Everywhere was dark and dreary and dead. If any stranger had come that way it was likely he would think he was following the black road to hell.

As soon as the laundry maid told Topaz that the marquis was back, she had started to wait for him again. She wasn't sure if he would come, but it never occurred to her not to go to the rock where they had met before.

When she saw him her heart contracted. She was wrapped in an old cloak which did little to ward off the elements, but she was oblivious to any discomfort.

She waited until he grew nearer and then walked up to him, her face alight.

Andrew felt like a drowning man. His marriage was only weeks away and the responsibility he felt for Virginia had grown more onerous when he saw the love in her. His life would be a charade, for every time he took her in his arms he would see the face of the girl now smiling at him in a way which lit fires in his heart.

"My lord, I was told you were back."

"For a while."

He was examining his gloves with scrupulous care, not wanting to see Topaz's disappointment.

"You are returning to London again?"

"In a few weeks."

"But I thought the season didn't start until May. I asked Mother Benedicta about it and it all sounded so exciting. But perhaps you are going for business reasons."

When he didn't reply she felt something bad approaching and tried to ward it off with an apology.

"I'm sorry. I didn't mean to pry. What you do in town is none of my business."

"No, it isn't, and I'm glad you realize it."

The sting was no longer there and then he knew he had to make the confession which would herald the end for them.

"Topaz, I'm going to marry again."

He waited, breath held in, to see how she would take it. She was very young and he knew how much she loved him. He was prepared for tears or temper or both, but she was very calm.

"I expected you would. You need an heir."

The wildness and stubborn valour in her had become real strength and it surprised him. It also made him want even more to pull her close and heal her wounds with a kiss.

"Yes, I do. My name cannot die with me."

"Of course not. Is she very pretty?"

It was a question so typically feminine that somehow it released part of the tension in him.

"Very."

"Has she got golden hair and blue eyes?"

"As a matter of a fact she has."

"I'm glad for you, my lord, but I expect that as you're so

rich you could have had any woman you wanted. It's not likely you'd pick an ugly one. Mother says money isn't important, but secretly I disagree with her. You might not have won a beauty if you were poor."

The child in her was uppermost again, as practical as ever.

"Perhaps not."

"You won't be riding up to High Tor any more, I suppose?"

It was a repetition of an earlier encounter. For the second time he should have said no, and for the second time he didn't.

"I probably will, just for a while, unless you'd rather I didn't."

Sloe eyes met aquamarine ones, so much passing between them without a single word being uttered.

"I'd like you to come," said Topaz finally. "As you say, it won't be for long."

"Wear something warmer to-morrow."

"I haven't got anything else."

"You can have my greatcoat."

As he began to unbutton it, Topaz laughed. It was a sound which had sent a thrill through him the first time he had heard it. It was no different now.

"And how can I explain such finery to Mother Benedicta?"

"I hadn't thought of that, but I hate to see you so cold."

"I'm not any more."

"Nevertheless, you'd better go. The Moor isn't kind to those lightly clad."

"There are other things more unkind, but it is time I went."

He wondered if he would feel her mouth against his again, but she turned away with a brief wave. He sighed, feeling cheated.

He had wanted her kiss. He also wanted to dress her in warm wraps, soft furs and the finest of leather boots. He longed to put silk and satin on her body, diamonds round her neck, and touch her ears and breast with expensive perfume. But none of these privileges were his. There was nothing he could do for her now or in the future.

He was going to lose her for good and was powerless to stop the inexorable wheel of Fortune from taking her from him. And it was no wonder that she hadn't touched his lips with hers.

In eight weeks' time he would be Virginia Grafton's husband.

* * *

When Timothy Amsterdam returned from Europe he soon found a way of meeting Topaz on the Moor. She greeted him with pleasure, for she had liked him from the start.

After the first occasion, Timothy managed to contrive other encounters, Topaz never suspecting that they were anything but happy chances.

She asked many questions about his travels, eager to know about all the places he had seen. In turn, she told him of her life under Benedicta's wing, making him laugh when she related her earlier antics and gave creditable impersonations of the good Sisters.

Timothy had heeded Aunt Agatha's suggestion that he should leave England for a while. At first he hadn't wanted to go, but in the end he had seen the sense of it and tried to put Topaz out of his mind.

As soon as he saw her again, however, he knew he was as much in love with her as ever, patient in his desire, for he knew she wouldn't have been cured of her passion for Andrew yet.

Then came the day when she explained about Yelton.

"A very worthy calling," he said, his heart sinking, for she seemed to be moving further away from him than ever. "But have you ever thought of another way of life?"

She frowned.

"Another way? What else could I do?"

"You could get married."

She stared at him for a moment, then grinned.

"I don't see how. I'm told most of the men at Yelton have one foot in the grave and if there are any young 'uns, Sister Beatrice would soon send them packing. She runs the House there. They say she's a tartar, but I won't mind that. I can be a tartar, too, can't I?"

"My God you can. You half-killed Andrew."

"He half-killed me, more like."

He returned to the subject of matrimony.

"Yelton isn't the only place on earth."

"It's the only place I'll be, 'cept here, and there's no one round about these parts who'd want me."

It was then that she looked into his eyes and went cold with shock. Hitherto, she'd thought of him as a friend; a kind friend, far above her station.

But there was no mistaking his message. She knew too much about unrequited love to misunderstand what she saw in him. She was caught off balance, frightened at first. But then she sensed he wasn't going to put his emotions into words just then. She was thankful for that, because it gave her time to think carefully about the extraordinary situation which had so unexpectedly arisen.

She had never considered an alternative to Yelton. Now she could choose second-rate happiness, cosseted and protected by a man who could give her anything she wanted, except the marquis. On the other hand, she could stick to her original plan, working like a slave but remaining faithful to Andrew in her heart.

"Yes," she said finally, "I suppose marriage is another way, but I don't want to think about that for a while."

Timothy was unperturbed. She was only seventeen. By the time she was nineteen or twenty she might have changed her views about such an austere future. He didn't mind how long he waited. He cared for her too much to be impatient.

"Did you know the marquis was getting married again?"

He didn't want to rub salt into her wounds. He just wanted to warn her how hopeless her case was.

She kept her chin up, her eyes blank.

"Yes. There's a girl who comes from the village to help at the convent. She knows everybody's business, especially the gentry's. I hope he'll be happy."

Silently he applauded her fortitude, wanting to hold her to give her the solace he knew she needed.

"I expect he will. Oh, do you have to go?"

"Yes and in a hurry. I'm dreadfully late and Sister Margaret will skin me alive. I'm supposed to be helping her to bake bread. I'm not very good at it, but she makes me try even though I keep burning it."

"A determined woman. Yes, you must get along, but we will see each other again, won't we?"

" 'Course we will. I'll bring you a loaf next time."

"I'd like that, charred though it may be."

She gave him a morsel of hope because he had always been so kind to her.

"I do like you, Mr. Amsterdam. I'm glad you're my friend. You are my friend, aren't you?"

She waved good-bye without waiting for an answer and Timothy sighed.

"Yes," he said aloud when she had gone. "But it's not what I want to be. Damn Yelton to hell! The place for you, my darling Topaz, is in my bed."

* * *

As soon as Topaz was nineteen, Mother Benedicta sent her to Yelton. Her charge was still spirited underneath, but had learned to wear a calm and gentler front, very composed as she went about her work. By then she had turned to God, every bit as fervent in her belief as the Sisters. Benedicta saw no point in waiting any longer.

"I think you're ready to begin your proper training," she said to Topaz when the latter had made her obeisance.

"You've learned a great deal from Sister Anne and I see in you the quality which is needed at Yelton. How do you feel about it?"

Topaz was delighted, but she didn't shew it in case Mother thought she was anxious to leave High Tor.

"I would like to go. I will miss you all, of course, but I want to start some real work."

"You'll be coming back here now and then; we shan't be saying good-bye to you. I think I should tell you something about Sister Beatrice."

Benedicta paused, not quite sure how to go on, but Topaz smiled.

"I have heard people speak of her, Mother. You have taught me discipline and I'm sure I will be able to serve her."

"I hope so. She's a fine nurse, but stands no nonsense from anyone. You won't be able to wear your earrings any more; those will have to stay in your pocket."

Topaz nodded and two days later set out with Sister Cecilia and Sister Anne, who were to be her escort. She had been given a plain black dress with a crisp white apron and a mob-cap. The thick coils of hair had been pinned up beneath it by a patient Sister Anne, who sighed as she went about her task.

"You look so different," she had said. "You're not a child any more."

"I haven't been for some time. And I'm no longer wayward." Topaz laughed. "It's just as well, dear Sister Anne, from what I've heard of my new mistress."

Yelton was a small but scattered village near the bleakest part of the Moor. More prosperous hamlets would have nothing to do with the inhabitants and, but for the Community's care, many would have starved or died prematurely.

The barn was stark and without adornment, save for a single crucifix in the tiny chapel. It was without a speck of dirt or grime, the old wooden floors white with constant scrubbing; the pallets on which the sick lay were furnished with coarse but spotlessly clean linen.

Sister Beatrice was a surprise. Topaz had pictured her as tall and brawny as befitted a martinet. But she was tiny, with a wrinkled face and steely grey eyes. She looked her new helper over and pursed her lips.

"I've heard about you," she said. "A hoyden and an atheist when you first got to High Tor."

Topaz made up her mind at once not to cringe from Beatrice. Amossy's granddaughter didn't fear anyone, but she wasn't impudent either. She had to deal with this woman, who could teach her what she wanted to know, and her voice was tranquil as she replied.

"Yes, Sister Beatrice, I was, but no longer. I have learned to love God and I will obey you in everything."

"You certainly will, or you'll find yourself packed off to Mother Benedicta very quickly."

But after that seemingly unpropitious start, Topaz settled into the routine at Yelton as if she had been there all her life. She worked untiringly, always patient and kind to the men, women and children whom she helped, eager to learn from her companions, and devout in her prayers.

After a few weeks, Beatrice sent for her.

"You had little sleep last night, Topaz, and hardly any the night before."

"I was busy, Sister Beatrice. We had a number of new patients, some of them children. They were frightened, so I stayed with them."

"I know precisely how many patients we receive here each day, but you are trying to cram a lifetime into a month or so. Slow down, my dear. You're doing well enough."

Topaz blushed with pleasure at the unexpected praise, but she still went on driving herself to, and beyond, her limits. It helped to keep her mind away from Andrew. When the laundry maid had told her he had been married, she had gone up to the high moors and wept. Then she had gone to Mother Benedicta and told her of her sin.

Benedicta hadn't judged.

"When you have been confirmed, you'll be able to make your confession," she'd said. "Meanwhile, put this man out of your heart and mind. He is another woman's husband now and to lust after him is sinful."

Topaz had tried hard to heed Benedicta's warning, but it was impossible. Andrew was always with her, walking a few steps out of her reach.

Her encounters with Timothy had continued and it was he who had told her of the birth of Andrew's son a year after his marriage. She had tried not to mind and was careful to shew nothing but pleasure. But that night she had knelt in her cell through the long, dark hours, begging the Almighty to forgive her for her envy and sadness.

When she went to Yelton, Timothy started to visit the Community, furnishing it with funds for its work. Sister Beatrice was an old friend of Lady Agatha's and accepted Amsterdam's frequent appearances without comment. She had strong feelings about the aristocracy playing a part in the care of those less fortunate than themselves and Timothy was charming to everyone. For once, Beatrice's eagle eye failed to detect the tenderness in Timothy whenever he spoke to Topaz.

When Spring came, Topaz was allowed to leave the outpost and go to the village itself to take food to the old and infirm. There were many of them, and the simple home-made bread, butter, honey and milk scarcely went around, despite Amsterdam's generosity.

She was walking back one day, her baskets empty, her spirit almost peaceful for once. It was a beautiful afternoon and Nature was colouring the Moor with breathtaking tints. A light breeze made play with her skirts and, for the first time since she had arrived at Yelton, she wished she could let down her hair and feel the wind run its fingers through it.

When she saw Andrew it seemed to her as if her heart had stopped beating. She had had no idea he was on

Dartmoor, for she never asked Timothy any questions about him. It was better not to know, then she didn't have to picture him with his wife and child in their London house, or at High Brook. Such scenes of domestic bliss would only turn to torments and she forced him to be a spectre at the back of her mind.

When the marquis came up to her the ghost fled. He was there in substance. Flesh and blood and so wonderful to look at. The sudden urgent needs of her body came from her gypsy roots; fiery, desperate and unquenchable. She forgot Mother Benedicta, High Tor, Beatrice and Yelton. All she could see was Andrew, and all she could feel was her longing for him.

Andrew looked down at her, healed by the mere sight of her. He wasn't unhappy with Virginia. She was a pleasant companion, but nothing more. Her devotion to him was touching, but he still didn't love her. Even his son, whom he worshipped, hadn't driven Topaz away.

They stood in silence for a few seconds; then they were in each other's arms.

"Oh, my dear," said Andrew after what seemed an eternity. "I promised myself I would never try to see you again. I know that I'm being unfair to you and to Virginia, but what I feel for you – what I have always felt for you – has made a weakling of me."

Topaz hadn't known what true contentment was until that moment. It was a state of existence so perfect that it almost frightened her because nothing perfect lasted for ever.

"I tried not to think of you either," she said. "I've worked until I've dropped so that I should fall asleep with exhaustion and not lie awake remembering you. I've loved you from that first day."

"I know." He took the mob-cap from her head, impatient with the pins until her hair fell past her shoulders like a black silk curtain. "I knew it was the same for you; that made it worse. God, let me hold you again."

Their bodies pressed close together, their lips hungry for the other's kisses. The marquis's strength made Topaz light-headed as they clung together, his desire a worthy match for hers.

"What would Mother Benedicta say if she could see us now?" Andrew released Topaz reluctantly. "She would think ill of me."

"And of me. She'd say we were committing a mortal sin, I expect."

"So we are."

"Then let us burn in hell for it." Topaz caught his hand. "I don't care what happens, or what anyone thinks of me, if I can be with you sometimes."

The marquis made one belated attempt to warn her.

"Think carefully, my sweet. I had a letter from Benedicta the other day. She gave a glowing report of your work and said you had become a Christian. If we end this now, the sin will rest with me. If we do meet again, you'll share the guilt."

"I won't mind that."

"I'll ride over as often as I can."

"And I'll be watching for you."

"We must take care that no one sees us."

"I know where the hidden places of the Moor are to be found."

He took her face between his hands, lost in the depths of her eyes.

"You should run from me," he said softly. "I am your destruction."

"You are my beloved and I won't run."

"Leave the Community, then neither of us will feel so badly about our treachery to Benedicta and the others. I'll buy you a house nearby."

She shook her head.

"No, the people of Yelton are very poor and need help, even from a sinner like me. To leave them would be another kind of running away."

"There will be many difficulties." He was still troubled. "You'll find yourself lying to those you care for. Hell! How damned selfish I'm being. I haven't the right to ask you to pay such a price."

She smiled, giving him comfort.

"Don't you understand, dearest? No price is too high just to feel your arms round me now and then. Our kind of loving isn't easy. There will be penalties for both of us to face. I'm ready to meet them. Are you?"

The shadow was still on Andrew as he replied.

"Yes, but I wish it didn't have to be like this. I want to share my whole life with you, openly and in freedom."

"But that isn't possible. Don't ask for too much, Andrew. The crumbs we have are very precious."

She blew the darkness away and he gave her a quick smile as the last doubt faded.

"You always had courage, Topaz Chilcott. I should have remembered that."

Their lips met once more as slowly they savoured the pure essence of love. Then Andrew made his way back to Nero, and Topaz began to pin up her hair.

As she walked back to the barn she thought about what the marquis had said. Benedicta, Anne, and their companions had given her their affection and trust and she was about to throw it back in their faces. Sooner or later she would have to stand before the Mother Superior and confess what she had done, but even that awful prospect couldn't quell her joy just then.

Andrew loved her, and nothing else in the whole world mattered to her as much as that.

* * *

"Timothy, it's time you got married."

Lady Agatha, very chic in a cambric high gown and lace cap, was firm as she fixed her nephew with an unwavering stare.

Amsterdam looked over the rim of his coffee cup, wondering what was going on inside the head of his august relation. He had no doubt that it was something devious, and her tone indicated she had already made her choice for him.

"She's right, Mr. Timothy." Fidelma should have left the room some five minutes before, but she was fiddling with the silver milk jug and sugar basin so that she didn't miss anything. "Every man needs a good woman, b'Jesus he does."

"Be quiet," snapped Lady Agatha. "This is none of your affair, and why are you still here?"

"Ah, that's 'cos you might forget something important you have to say, and ask for my help."

"Hell will freeze over before that's likely to happen." Agatha turned back to Amsterdam. "Now, since you haven't found anyone in London to suit your taste, what about that nice West girl who's always sighing over you?"

Timothy was jolted out of his normal equilibrium.

"Honor? Sighing over me? Dearest, for once you've been misinformed. We've known each other since we were infants, but she doesn't have that kind of feeling for me."

The two women looked at each other in exasperation.

"She's been head over heels in love with you for ages," said Lady Agatha impatiently. "Really! Some men seem to be born blind."

"All of 'em are." Fidelma put her pennyworth in before she was finally banished. "They wouldn't see a four-leafed clover if they fell over it."

"We're not discussing vegetation, you maddening old fool. Will you go away and let me have a serious discussion with my nephew without these constant interruptions? My dear, I know what I'm talking about. Many people have noticed how she looks at you. I had hoped for someone a little more – well – never mind. Honor is really quite suitable."

"Provided you didn't marry 'er ma as well, that is."

"Fiddy!"

"I'm going, I'm going. But what Lady Agatha says is true, Mr. Timothy. I know one of the maids who works for Lady West, unfortunate girl that she is – the maid, I mean. She says Lady West is always telling Miss Honor she's got no hope with you, and that the poor lass cries herself to sleep most nights."

Fidelma stumped out of the room, deciding she had pressed her luck far enough and Timothy put his cup down, oddly disturbed.

"Be honest with me about this. Never mind whether you think I need a wife or not. Does Honor care about me like that?"

"I never lie, and I'll thank you to remember it."

"You've been known to bend the truth when it suits you, but I must be sure this time."

Agatha stopped glaring at her nephew.

"Yes, it's true. She's loved you for years. I wouldn't deceive you about anything as important as this. Good God, boy, you may be bereft of sight, but I'm not."

Amsterdam was frowning, suddenly recalling the number of social occasions when Honor had contrived to be at his elbow. It made him sad, for he was fond of her.

"Well?"

He took a deep breath.

"Well what? If you are asking whether I feel the same about her, the answer is no. I'd never considered her as a wife."

"Perhaps you'd better do so now."

"It's not possible."

"Because you're still thinking about that girl who works with beggars and ne'er-do-wells at Yelton, I suppose! I know you've been up there a lot lately. You're a cretin; she's not for you. She's a gypsy. She may work with the Sisters of St. Francis, but she's still a tinker."

"Half-Romany," he replied softly, "and a beautiful woman. I see now why you're so anxious to get me married off to Honor. I'll tell you something, Aunt Ag."

Agatha didn't like the expression in Timothy's eyes. It was as if he were gazing into heaven, and Agatha wasn't so old that she'd forgotten what that felt like.

"What?"

Amsterdam rose and put his hand on his aunt's shoulder as if to soften the blow he was about to deliver.

"I will love Topaz as long as my life lasts and, if I can't have her, I won't marry at all. I'm sorry, but that is how it is. She is the only woman in the world for me. Perhaps you'd better get Fiddy to say some prayers for me. I rather think I'm going to need them."

Five

The last two years had gone by very slowly for Honor West. She had managed to keep her mother, and the persistent George Chambers, at bay but with increasing difficulty.

She had wept when Timothy had gone abroad, but his return had not improved matters. She seldom saw him and certainly he never sought her out.

It was her mother who had told her about Timothy's frequent visits to the village of Yelton, and Tipper who had confirmed her mistress's story, adding that Amsterdam was a gormless idiot and Topaz Chilcott a dirty slut.

Honor had had no idea that there was a woman in Timothy's life and the news had taken every vestige of colour out of her face. Her hands had trembled as they tried to re-fill Lady West's cup and the latter had been quick to press home her advantage.

"There, what did I tell you? It's no use you waiting about for him. He's got other things on his mind."

"A common tinker, too, m'lady." Tipper had pretended to be shocked, but she had enjoyed the sight of Honor's shattered composure. "You'd think he'd look higher than that, wouldn't you?"

Honor had prayed that her mother and Ida had been lying, but Mrs. Luke, Lady West's dressmaker, confirmed the tale.

"Aye, Miss Honor, it's true enough. Got a cousin living just outside Yelton. She says folk tell how sweet he is on her. Right smitten, poor man. Some women have no decency in them."

Every now and then when Lady Flora wanted to talk scandal with her friends, Honor was allowed to go riding. One day she turned North to Yelton, not sure what she was going to do when she got there. She just knew she had to see the woman who held Timothy's heart and perhaps persuade her to set him free.

When she reached the village she was shocked by the sight of the inhabitants. They looked so pale and pinched and thin. It was no wonder the good Sisters had come to such a place to work. But why a hot-blooded gypsy, presumably with no belief in God, should want to do so, too, was a puzzle.

She asked where Topaz could be found and was directed to the barn. Then she saw an elderly Sister and made another enquiry.

"Yes, my child, she's in our living quarters, just back there. Knock on the second door you come to. God be with you."

But knocking on the second door she came to wasn't as easy as it sounded. Honor felt her mouth go dry and her knees begin to shake. What could she possibly say to a beauty with thick hair down to her waist, wearing bright clothes, and gold bracelets up her arm?

Topaz Chilcott would give her a sly look. She'd been told by Tipper, who wouldn't leave the subject alone, that all tinkers were sly. They swore, too, Ida had said, needing their mouths washed out with strong soap and water.

In the end, Honor gritted her teeth and tapped on the door. It was a second or two before it opened and when it did her lips parted silently.

The occupant of the hut, for it was no more than that, wore a shabby but neat uniform, an apron, and a cap which concealed every strand of hair. Honor thought she was the most exquisite girl she had ever seen and her heart sank lower than ever. It was no wonder that Timothy was in love with her; any man would be. She was about to turn away without a word when Topaz said gently:

"Please come in and sit down. You look so tired. I haven't much to offer you, I'm afraid, but the water from the spring near here is very pure."

Honor found herself pressed to take the only available chair, grateful for the cool liquid which quenched her thirst and gave her time to regain at least some of her self-possession.

"I'm Honor West," she said hesitantly. "You must think it very strange of me to come here without warning. You don't even know who I am."

Topaz saw the misery in her visitor's eyes and remembered that once Timothy had mentioned Lady West and her daughter. There had been no emotion in his voice when he had spoken Honor's name. It was clear that to him she was just a playmate of years long gone.

"I have heard Mr. Amsterdam talk of you and your mother." Topaz was cautious, because she was beginning to understand what was wrong with Miss West. "I believe you are old friends."

"He thinks of me as such." Honor still couldn't quite believe what she was seeing. There was such peace in the eyes which were looking so honestly into hers. No slyness, no curses. Just a compassionate girl working amongst dirt and poverty. "Only as that, I'm afraid."

"And you?"

Honor looked down at her gloves and began to fiddle with the buttons.

"I shouldn't have come. What will you think of me?"

"Only that you are unhappy and probably care for Mr. Amsterdam in quite a different way."

"I must go; I'm going to cry."

"Then cry here. It isn't good to weep alone."

Topaz saw how the sobs shook Honor's body and wanted to hold her like a child to comfort her. But she had to be careful. Timothy, although a regular caller, hadn't mentioned the alternative to Yelton again, but the way he looked at her from time to time made words unnecessary.

"Do you feel better?"

Honor straightened up and mopped her eyes.

"Not really, although I'm grateful to you for your tolerance. I've made a complete fool of myself and I don't think I can bring myself to ask what I came to do."

"Why not? You haven't been foolish. Sometimes tears help."

"Not to-day, I'm afraid. I hadn't expected you to be a bit as you are."

Topaz's laugh was warm and Honor felt some of the ice inside her begin to melt.

"You pictured me in gaudy skirts, dangling earrings and necklace, dancing round a camp fire? Well, I did wear them once, and now and then I danced, but not often. My family didn't like me so I had to work hard."

Suddenly it seemed to Honor that a bond was being forged between them.

"My mother doesn't like me either."

"What about your father?"

"He's dead. I have to work hard as well."

"There, we have that much in common. Ask your question, Miss West."

Honor coloured.

"It wasn't exactly a question and now I know what

you're like I don't think I can –"

"Try. Don't let whatever it is fester. What is it you want of me?"

Honor said rapidly:

"I want you to go away, because I've been told that Timothy is in love with you. He'll never see me while you are here and no one could blame him, for you are so lovely. I'm just plain and uninteresting and I can't compete with you, but I do want him so very much. I've wanted him for as long as I can remember."

Topaz tried to avoid the direct lie, deeply sorry for the girl with the blotched face and red eyes.

"Mr. Amsterdam has never said anything to me which was out of place and I can't leave. My work is here."

"You could ask to be moved to another convent."

For a second Topaz thought of Andrew. Then she said regretfully:

"No, I can't do that, but I am no threat to you."

"But you are. He'll ask you to marry him."

"He hasn't done so yet."

"He will, I know he will. Miss Chilcott, don't stay in Yelton."

"I have to. This isn't something which can be forced, you know. If Mr. Amsterdam loves you, it won't matter where I am."

"But he doesn't and it will matter." Honor slumped back in her chair defeated. "If you remain, all he will ever see is you."

"I wish I could put your world to rights for you."

"You could, if you did as I ask of you. Do you want me to beg? I will, if that's what you require of me. You see, I have no shame, no pride."

"No, I don't ask you to beg, and my going isn't the answer."

"It's the only way I know."

"Was Mr. Amsterdam very attentive to you before I came?"

Honor shook her head.

"No, but there's always a chance for a new start without you."

Honor got up like an old woman, glancing past Topaz to the shelves where bottles of medicine were stored.

"So much healing in those," she said drearily. "So many panaceas. What a pity there isn't something there to cure the sickness of a love which isn't returned. It does hurt so and I'm not sure how much longer I can bear the pain.

"Oh, Miss Chilcott, please, please go away."

* * *

That autumn the barn at Yelton began to fall down. At first, the Sisters themselves tried knocking in a few nails or propping up walls with staves. When that didn't halt the disintegration they got a few able-bodied men from the village to help, but after a while it was obvious that much more radical repair was needed.

It became clear that if the Community's work was to continue, they would need money and thus the Sisters went out begging in other villages, and visiting the gentry in their mansions scattered about that part of the Moor.

When Topaz arrived at the residence of Lord Oswin Lovat she didn't hold out much hope of prising his purse open. He was known to be a bad-tempered recluse, avoided by everyone in the area. A wizened butler opened the door to Topaz, but it took five minutes of heated argument before she was allowed to step over the threshold of Stone Towers.

She thought the place well-named, for the hall was bleak and comfortless and as cold as winter on High Tor.

Her first sight of Lovat wasn't encouraging either. He was in his library, lolling back in a chair by the hearth. He was very stout, his breeches like a second skin, his waistcoat straining across his belly. Topaz searched his face for some indication that her mission would be successful, but she found no hint of benevolence.

His cheeks were full and the colour of the port of which he was so fond. His eyes were small, but as shrewd as any Topaz had seen and she knew she wouldn't be able to gull him.

"Well, what d'yer want?" He didn't waste time on small talk. "Damned impertinence comin' here disturbin' a man in his own castle. Speak up, girl, or I'll have Roberts throw you out."

Topaz could feel her blood beginning to boil, but she clenched her hands by her sides and kept her voice even.

"I've come to ask you for money, my lord. The barn at Yelton, belonging to the Sisters of St. Francis, needs much spent on it and we haven't anything left. If we can't raise funds we shall have to close it and then the villagers will starve or die of disease."

"Good thing, too. They're a lot of idle beggars and there are too many people in the world anyway."

Topaz said a Hail Mary and part of the Lord's Prayer; then she lost her temper. All that Mother Benedicta had taught her, and every ounce of self-discipline dinned into her by Sister Beatrice, flew to the four winds. She was pure Romany as she pulled off her cap, flung it to the floor, and stamped her foot.

"You disgusting, bloated, selfish old man. How dare you speak of other human beings like that? You haven't gone short of food, that's obvious. You're like a bladder of lard. Any one of the souls to whom we give succour is worth ten like you. You ought to go to Yelton yourself and see the privation there, but I don't suppose you could walk as far as your gate, never mind finding a horse strong enough to carry you. Aristocrat you may be; pig you certainly are. Now call your butler and let him try and lay hands on me."

Lovat was used to cringing servility, and he couldn't remember when anyone had last disagreed with him, never mind treating him to a scalding tirade of abuse. He watched open-mouthed when his attacker's black hair shed its pins as she shook with rage, dumbfounded by the eyes which were hotter than the fire by which he sat.

It amazed him such a slip of a girl could have such passion in her, and by then he had noticed the perfect contours of her body which neither the black dress nor the prim white apron could conceal. It made him regret the passing of his youth, and the ennui he had felt before her arrival had miraculously disappeared.

"Damn me," he said finally. "You saucy chit. Never tell me you're one of those pie-bald vultures who interferes with Nature's design of life and death by forcing gruel down the throats of those who belong in the grave?"

"No I'm not, but I work with them. And don't call them names or I'll tear your cheek open."

Oswin sniggered.

"Egad, you've got spirit, I'll say that for you. What's your name?"

"Topaz Chilcott, but that's neither here nor there."

"Topaz, eh? Sounds pagan; better still. I like it."

"You're not asked to like it or dislike it," she retorted curtly. "Are you going to give me something or not? I haven't got all day to waste on you."

"Not so much of a hurry." Oswin stirred in his chair and winced. The termagant was right; he was getting rather overweight. "I want to know more about you. Come to think of it, I did hear that those nuns had caught themselves a gypsy. That's you, I suppose?"

"Yes, but that isn't your business either."

"Don't be so sure about that. I've no patience with pious, sexless females, but I'm quite taken by Romanies. Colourful, even if the whole pack of 'em are thieves."

"At least you didn't call me a tinker, and they're not all thieves."

"Most of 'em are. I'll think about what you're asking for. Come back next week, if you dare, and I'll give you my answer."

Topaz picked up her cap, still seething.

"Don't worry, my lord, I dare, and I'll be back. I'm not

frightened of you."

She was as good as her word, walking into the library ready to give Lovat another piece of her mind. The wind was taken out of her sails in the first two minutes when Oswin handed her a hundred pounds.

"Here, build yourself some good foundations and a stout wall or two. Come back next week, same time. Never know; I might give you some more."

Topaz walked down Lovat's drive in a daze. Sister Beatrice would be delighted, particularly if more largesse were to follow. Topaz knew she would have to make her confession concerning her lost temper, but it was worth a penance. Anything was worth keeping the work going at Yelton.

After that she went to see Lovat regularly. They wrangled interminably, he goading her into outbursts of anger just to watch her beauty at its best, she calling him all the names she could lay her tongue to.

It wasn't long before visiting Stone Towers became part of her life. Sister Beatrice, under the impression that Topaz was bringing out the hitherto suppressed goodness in Lovat, encouraged her. Not for a second did the notion cross Beatrice's mind that Lovat was having carnal thoughts which he knew could never be fulfilled. Nor did she suspect that every Thursday Topaz shed her humility and piety and swore at Oswin in a language the words of which Beatrice wouldn't begin to understand.

By winter, a real affection had developed between Lovat and Topaz. It was never put into words, nor did it entirely dampen their blistering exchanges. But slowly the quarrels grew further and further apart as Oswin taught Topaz to play chess, throw the dice, and handle a pack of cards like an expert.

The Yelton outpost was saved, for Oswin's generosity increased as time went by. He waited anxiously for Topaz's arrival, bored when she wasn't there. Now and then Topaz felt some guilt. Gambling wasn't exactly the purpose for which Sister Beatrice had sent her to Stone Towers, but she shrugged off her misgivings. She had already fallen into sin by meeting Andrew in remote places whenever she could. The odd game of faro and whist was nothing compared with the kisses she shared with the marquis.

"Penny for 'em," said Lovat one afternoon when they were playing faro.

Topaz shrugged.

"Not worth that."

"Might be to me. What were you thinking about?"

"The fact that I'm a fallen woman."

"Because you're playing cards? God, those narrow-minded harpies have addled your brain. No harm in faro and hazard."

"It's not only that."

"What then?"

"I can't tell you, at least, not now."

Lord Lovat saw the unhappiness in his newly-found friend, but he knew the rules of the game and didn't press.

"Just as you like. Still, if you want an ear not stuffed up with prayers and platitudes, remember I'm here."

"I will." Topaz gave him a smile which made him quiver pleasurably. "I'll remember, and thank you. I'm sorry I once called you a pig."

"My hide's thick enough; it didn't bother me. If I'm not a pig, what am I?"

Topaz leaned forward and put her hand over Oswin's.

"You're a dear and kind gentleman and I wish you were my father."

Lovat hooted with mirth.

"That's a back-handed compliment if ever I heard one. Come on, you've gabbled enough and you're just trying to put me off my game. But I'll tell you this, Topaz Chilcott. I'm glad you're not my daughter. Who in the name of Hades wants to play cards with his daughter? I like things as they are. Now get on and deal, you minx. This is one game I'm going to win."

* * *

Andrew's nightmare began one dark November day. He hadn't been able to see Topaz for over two weeks because Virginia had been ill. The doctor shook his head over the marchioness and, even now, when she had managed to leave her bed, a hard cough continuously racked her thin frame.

He was staring out of the drawing-room window when he became conscious of people talking in the hall. Then one voice grew louder, piercing into his brain as his body became paralyzed with shock and disbelief.

He turned, but before he could take a step the door opened and Horatia was there. He felt as if the floor were shifting under his feet, giddy as he tried to take in what was happening.

"Horatia?"

It was a whisper of sound, full of doubt.

"Yes, of course. Did you think I was a ghost? Well, you might say you're glad to see me but, in view of what I've heard, perhaps you're not."

Somehow Andrew managed to steady himself. Horatia was right. She wasn't a ghost. She was flesh and blood and terribly, terribly alive.

"But – but you went down in Foxton Mire. Two men saw you. They came to tell me that you'd gone under before they could help you. They told the inquest the same thing. Timothy and I went to search for you, but you weren't there."

"I never was." The marchioness loosened her mantle of grey cloth and threw it over a chair. "I paid those moormen very well to tell that story. Clibber and Butterworth; how odd that I can still remember their names. They didn't want to do it; they were as nervous as kittens, but in the end my offer was too good to turn down. I'm chilled to the bone. Give me some brandy, will you?"

The marquis managed to pour the brandy without spilling it, his face chalk-white as the ramifications of Horatia's return began to dawn on him.

"It was a lie? You didn't get trapped in the mire?"

"Of course not. Really, Andrew, isn't that obvious?"

"Then where were you?"

"On the coast road with the Comte de Michelet." Horatia sipped her drink, her voice suddenly brittle. "I was bored with you and this mausoleum. I wanted life, excitement and love. Also, I was very drunk.

"I hadn't intended to stay away long, of course; certainly not long enough for you to find yourself another wife. I sold the jewels I was wearing and de Michelet and I had a splendid time until the money was gone. After that, he went, too."

"Why didn't you come back then?"

Horatia pulled a face.

"Because something happened to stop me; I'll explain in a minute. Then, just as I was ready to leave for England I met John Leinster."

Andrew saw something in Horatia's face he had never seen before. The eyes were soft and dreamy, her lips tremulous. For a moment she looked as vulnerable as Virginia had ever done.

"Leinster?"

"Yes, you wouldn't know him. He's a nobody, but you see I fell in love with him. I would have done anything for him; gone anywhere with him. I didn't believe such happiness was possible and I was ready to make any sacrifice for him. I thought he felt the same about me; perhaps he did in the beginning. But in the end he was like all the rest. I found out that he was having an *affaire* with another woman. I pleaded with him not to leave me. Can you imagine that, Rossmayne? I actually went down on my knees and begged, but he laughed and threw me out. That was when I knew I had to come back. I was very short of funds, so I had no choice."

"But how could you let me go on thinking you were dead? When you met this man you say you loved, surely you could have told me."

She took another sip, the shallow blue eyes hard again.

"I knew you would try to find me. The family honour and all that nonsense. John never knew who I was; I gave him a false name. But if you'd come after me, and I'm sure you would have done, you'd have dragged me back to England and I didn't want to leave Leinster."

"Certainly I should have come to see you, but not necessarily forced you to return with me. I'm not that enamoured of you."

She shot him an unfriendly glance.

"I'm well aware of that, but you'd have had no choice. You see, seven months after I left England I had your son."

"What!"

"That shook you, my lord, didn't it? It rather shook me when I discovered I was pregnant by you."

"How do you know it's mine, you promiscuous – "

"Wait until you see him. There's no doubt; he's yours. And when you found I'd had your heir, you'd have brought me home fast enough."

"But you knew I'd remarried?"

"Yes, I'd heard. Connell was very useful. She kept in touch with me through someone else, who needn't concern you."

"My son – where is he?"

"Outside in the hall."

Andrew's head was nearly bursting with the deadly anger in him, half-suffocated by it as he became aware that someone else was in the room.

It was the most awful moment of his life and he didn't know how to handle it. Somehow he regained his self-control, forcing himself to speak normally.

"Virginia? Are you all right? You should be in bed."

Virginia was staring at Horatia, her lips almost blue, her pupils so dilated that the eyes looked black.

"It's true then." She moved towards Andrew, seeking his arm for support. "Connell told me, but I didn't think it could be so. Andrew!"

"Good God, Rossmayne, is this who you chose to take my place?" Horatia was caustic. "I can't pretend to admire your taste. She looks half-dead."

Virginia whimpered and the marquis's hold on her tightened.

"Be quiet, Horatia," he said and there was real venom in his voice. "Haven't you done enough already?"

"I've hardly started. My maid tells me you have a son, too, madam. Pity he's illegitimate."

"Hold your tongue." Andrew was feeling sick, but he had to stay strong for Virginia's sake. "I thought you frivolous, malicious and heartless when I lived with you. I never realized just how evil you really are. Can't you see what you've done by playing such a trick on me and staying away so long?"

"Of course I can see, but you can blame Leinster for that." Horatia trembled over the name. "But for him, I'd be out of your life for good. If he'd been faithful, I'd have stayed with him for ever and you and your paramour could have continued your idyllic existence." The moment of weakness was gone, her voice harsh once more. "Now you must meet Curtis."

Andrew and Virginia watched numbly as Horatia went to the door, returning a moment or two later with a small boy with silver-gold hair and eyes the colour of aquamarines. Virginia gave a cry, but Andrew was staring at the child hypnotised. It was like looking into a mirror.

"This is Curtis," said Horatia blandly. "Why don't you say hallo to him?"

It was while Horatia was pushing the boy forward that Virginia fainted. She didn't fall heavily, but lightly, as if a piece of muslin was drifting down to the carpet.

Over her supine body Andrew and Horatia's eyes met and she took the initiative, knowing she had to get the better of the marquis straight away.

"This is your heir, and I am your wife," she said gratingly. "Get that whore and her bastard out of my house. I never want to see either of them again. Do you hear, my lord? Get rid of them now."

* * *

Virginia died at midnight. The doctor had been sent for immediately she collapsed, but there was nothing he could do to save her. Her heart had failed and she hadn't regained consciousness since she was carried from the drawing-room. Andrew, sitting by her bed, holding one icy hand in his, thought that at least was a blessing.

"Convenient," said Horatia later. "That's one complication out of the way."

The lines round the corners of the marquis's mouth were deeply etched.

"The death of any human being is hardly convenient. And how do you propose to explain your prolonged absence? Are you going to tell the truth and shew the world what a strumpet you are?"

"Of course not." On the surface Horatia was very much mistress of the situation. Inside, she was bleeding from the wounds inflicted by John Leinster, for she loved him as much as ever. "I've had plenty of time to think of what I shall tell people.

"I shall explain that a certain man was mad for me, and was plaguing me to run away with him. Of course I refused with much indignation, and he grew very angry. I didn't tell you about this monster because I was afraid you would kill him and I thought I could handle the matter. In the end I found I couldn't.

"Foolishly, I dined with him to make clear that I wouldn't see him again and that if he persisted with his unwanted attention I would have no choice but to go to you. He slipped something in my wine and the next thing I knew was that we were on the Continent. I told him you would not let things rest and would look for me. He said you'd have no idea where to start and, in any event, he had bribed two shepherds to say I'd gone down to Foxton Mire.

"Ah, that reminds me. I must see Butterworth and Clibber to-morrow and give them some more money. They'll be petrified when they hear I'm home."

"You won't have to pay them a penny. They both died last year when a barn caught fire."

"Really? You see how splendidly things are fitting together? However, to go on. Suddenly the man went berserk. His face was scarlet and twisted with hate and he began to attack me like a wild animal. I thought he was going to tear me limb from limb. I must have fainted, and when I came to I didn't know who I was or where I'd come from."

Horatia was smiling to herself, pleased with the web of lies she was weaving.

"An Italian doctor delivered our son, for there were complications, and that part is the truth. I sounded him out about loss of memory. He said it could follow an incident so dire that the mind had to block it out, sometimes along with other things. I asked if he would swear a statement to this effect if it were necessary. He looked at me oddly until I named the price I would pay him."

The marquis was having difficulty keeping his hands off Horatia.

"I thought you had no money," he said shortly. "How could you bribe this man?"

"I had one necklace left. I wasn't such a fool as to let de Michelet sell everything." For a second her eyes looked moist. "I didn't even tell John I'd got it." Then she was herself again, brisk as she went on. "The emeralds fetched enough to gain the physician's goodwill and to pay for board and passage back to England when I was ready.

"But to continue with my tale of woe. The man had run off and I was with child. The woman with whom we boarded took pity on me and I worked in the house with her. I had flashes of recall and so many times seemed to be on the verge of knowing who I really was. Then things slipped away again. After the boy was born I returned to my work. Towards the end I began to get more and more glimpses into my past and at last my wits were fully restored.

"Naturally, I returned to my home and husband, where I belonged. I don't remember the man's name, but I don't suppose that matters, do you?"

"Very thin, madam."

"Do you think so?" Horatia yawned. "I thought it rather good. Some may have doubts, I suppose, but most will accept it. Why shouldn't they? They can't prove anything to the contrary and who is there hereabouts who knows anything about loss of memory and how long such a state lasts? The gossip will soon die down now that that woman is dead. We can stay on Dartmoor for some time boring though it is. It'll all be forgotten by the time we do go back to town.

"You'll have to back me up; you've no choice now that you have an heir to consider. As for that bastard – "

Andrew took three steps towards Horatia and caught her shoulders in a grip which made her cry out.

"Listen to me," he said softly. "That 'bastard', as you call him, is my son. He is as much my flesh and blood as Curtis is and he's going to stay here. Thanks to you, I cannot give him my name, but I shall furnish him with everything else he needs, including love. And you, you bitch, will accept him, too. Never mention his leaving here again, or God help you."

For the first time in her life Horatia was terrified of Rossmayne. There was insanity in his eyes, and she knew without a doubt that at that moment he wanted to murder her.

"All right, all right, he can stay. But you will support my story?"

"I've no choice, and I suppose losing one's memory is feasible in certain circumstances. When you meet

Virginia's parents, you will treat them with utmost kindness and regret, do you hear? And just remember your lines as if you were on the stage at Drury Lane. Don't refer to happenings during that period or this whole fabrication will fall like a pack of cards.

"And, madam." The marquis hadn't finished and Horatia began to shake in his hold. "Never mention Virginia to me, nor call her foul names in my hearing, or I will thrash you until you scream for mercy, and mercy you will not get. She was a kind and gentle girl and I cared for her greatly. You've taken her life; you will not take her reputation, too, do you understand me?"

Horatia swallowed hard.

"Yes – yes, my lord."

"Then go to your room. Perhaps to-morrow I shall be able to look at you and keep my hands from your throat. Get out, you trollop, get out!"

Horatia fled and Rossmayne went back to the window where he had been standing when the bad dream had begun.

"Dear Virginia," he said quietly, as if she were still by his side. "I'm so sorry, so very sorry. Please forgive me, for I shall never be able to forgive myself."

Then his face suddenly contorted until it was a livid mask.

"Damn you, Horatia," he said through set teeth. "I wish you were really at the bottom of Foxton Mire, or burning in the fires of Hell. Christ, you she-devil! Why aren't you dead?"

Six

Three days later, Timothy rode to Yelton to tell Topaz what had happened and of the story which the marchioness had concocted.

"She plays her rôle well," he said sourly. "Everyone

accepts her tale. She has luck on her side, too. Virginia's doctor, a self-important little man, had a patient once who lost her memory after the shock of seeing her husband fall to his death over a cliff. He considers himself an expert on the subject now and confirms that what Horatia says is entirely possible."

"No one blames Andrew for marrying again?"

"No, no. An inquest declared Horatia dead. Andrew had every right to assume he was free to take another wife."

Topaz grieved for Andrew and for Virginia, the girl she had never met, but of whom Timothy had said many kind things.

"It's a good thing Rossmayne is strong," said Amsterdam, still very troubled by the dark emotions which had been unleashed a night or two before. Horatia had always looked petulant; now she looked vengeful and he was sure her mischief wasn't finished. She had been scorned by Leinster and, if he knew anything about her, someone was going to pay for that. There was a whisper amongst the servants that she had fled from Andrew in terror on the night of her return. That was something else for which Horatia would exact payment in due course. "It's enough to drive a man to insanity."

"It was a dreadful thing to do. Has the marchioness no remorse?"

"She doesn't know the meaning of the word. She knew Andrew had married again. It seems Connell got messages through to her somehow. At the time, Horatia didn't care; she had what she wanted. Now she's been thrown over by Leinster she's the Marchioness of Rossmayne again. Andrew should have got rid of Connell when Horatia disappeared. He never liked the woman, but when she wept and begged him not to turn her out he weakened. He should have pitched her into Foxton Mire and saved himself a lot of trouble. Now she's fawning over her mistress again and whatever plans Horatia has, you may be sure Connell will help her. They are a pair well-matched."

Topaz wished she could see Andrew and comfort him, but for the time being that would be too dangerous. She would have to wait and see whether he wanted their meetings to continue, or whether he wished to turn his back on his previous life and start another.

"After all I've learned from Mother Benedicta about forgiveness I know I ought not to wish the marchioness ill, but she does deserve to be punished, doesn't she? She really is wicked."

Timothy looked straight into Topaz's eyes and in that split second she knew without doubt that he was aware of her love for Andrew.

He said slowly:

"Yes, she's wicked, but more than that. She is dangerous, Topaz; never forget that."

She accepted his warning without comment, but she took it to heart.

Horatia Manners was dangerous and she, Topaz, had to remember it.

* * *

A week later, Timothy Amsterdam asked Topaz to marry him.

"I know you don't feel about me as I do about you, but that doesn't matter." He gave a lop-sided grin. "It sounds trite, but I have enough love for both of us to live on."

Topaz had dreaded the moment since she first realized what Timothy had been working up to. He was such a good man and she was so fond of him. There seemed no way of refusing him without causing him hurt.

"I'm very flattered," she said nervously, picking her words with care. "Any woman would be honoured to be your wife."

"Now you're being trite. I don't want compliments; I want you. I worship the ground you walk on, you must know that by now."

"I didn't mean to put it so awkwardly. I just don't know how to tell you – "

" – that you're in love with Andrew! Yes, I've known that for a long time. It doesn't make any difference to me."

It was out in the open now and she was able to look him in the face again, all pretence finished.

"I realized you know," she said. "I saw it in your eyes the other day when you warned me about the marchioness. I'm sorry."

"So am I, for your sake. My dear, Andrew can never be yours."

"I know. I don't mind that."

"But you should. Your life will be barren and it shouldn't be. I can look after you, care for you, take you away from sickness and death."

"I'm not afraid of those things. They're part of my work."

"They don't have to be. You don't have to work at all."

She said nothing and a moment or two of silence fell on them like one of the Moor's deadly mists.

"I see," he said finally, "but please don't say no at once. Think about it for a few days, that's all I ask of you. Give me that much hope, Topaz."

She couldn't deny him, her voice husky as she gave him her promise. Life was so perverse. Timothy was agonising over her, when Honor West would have sold her soul for a single kiss from him. She, Topaz, would love Andrew whilst she still drew breath, but he was imprisoned at High Brook with a wife he loathed.

"Thank you." Amsterdam was pulling on his gloves, smiling at her as if everything was all right with his world, keeping his tribulation to himself. "I shall live on hope for the next week.

"Dearest Topaz; I wonder if you have any idea what you mean to me."

* * *

"Do you think Mr. Timothy's asked that gypsy to marry

him yet?" Fidelma O'Brien was brushing her mistress's hair with vigour. "He said if he couldn't have her, he wouldn't marry at all. He's been that sad the last few days."

"I had noticed, and stop tugging my hair so hard, you clumsy wretch."

"Do you reckon he'd tell us if he had proposed?"

Agatha studied her reflection in the looking-glass, aware that there were new lines round her eyes and mouth. She was paler, too. She'd never had a day's illness in her life, but Timothy's future was beginning to prey on her mind. It made her head ache and there had been a kind of knot in her stomach ever since her nephew had made his absurd announcement.

"He'd have to eventually, wouldn't he? Don't be so stupid."

"Wonder if she'll accept him."

"Why shouldn't she?" Lady Agatha was acid. "Good-looking, plenty of money, and doting on her. What woman could refuse all that?"

"One whose heart was somewhere else, maybe."

"Andrew Manners? Yes, I'd thought about him, but he can't wed her, can he? He's already had a surfeit of wives. What girl would want to go on working amongst those unfortunates when they could have the comfort of Timothy's home?"

"A strong-minded colleen with a sense of right and wrong."

"She's a Romany, not a colleen, and even if those nuns have taught her right from wrong, the temptation is too much."

"You going to say anything to him? Try to talk him out of it, like?"

"What's the use? You heard what he said. It's that girl or no one. Oh leave it, leave it! I'll be as bald as a coot if you go on like that. If you need exercise, go and scrub a floor."

"It's Miss West I'm sorry for." Fidelma ignored the

reprimand and the invitation to do some housework. "Still cryin' over him, I'm told."

"What a mess, and your prayers have done no good." Slowly Agatha got up, feeling twinges in her joints which hadn't been there before. "Your saints are nothing more than a lot of mischief-makers."

As Fidelma got Agatha into bed, they looked at each other with honesty as they always did in the end. The grumbles and complaints meant nothing. It was their way of communicating.

"I'm sorry," said Fidelma quietly, patting the coverlet with a meaty hand. "I'm truly sorry, m'lady."

"So am I, Fiddy, so am I. Oh, go and get us both a glass of brandy, woman. I think I'm going to cry."

* * *

When Topaz went to see Lord Lovat that week she was unusually silent. He endured the situation for ten minutes, then he grew tetchy.

"What's wrong with you to-day? You haven't said more than two words since you got here."

"There's nothing the matter with me." Her denial was swift and patently false. "I'm really quite all right."

"Liar. I shall go on bullying you until you tell me what's amiss."

Topaz hesitated. There was so much to tell, and she didn't know how to explain the tangle in a way which made sense. Some things seemed too intimate to share, and she would have to speak of secrets which were not her own.

On the other hand, Lovat's never-failing common sense would be a boon. He had a clear, incisive mind and might be able to blow some of the cobwebs away so that she knew what to say to Amsterdam when the time came.

"I don't want to burden you with my problems."

"So you've got problems, have you? Not the same as those you ranted on about the day we first met?"

She tried to smile, but the effort failed.

"No, not like those. These are personal."

"I thought as much. Get 'em off your chest; you'll feel better for it and I've a broad back."

"I don't know where to start."

"Try the beginning."

"All right, but first I'd like to know if you've heard of the return of the Marquis of Rossmayne's first wife and the death of his second."

"Of course I've heard. That's stale news. Horatia's supposed to have lost her memory during the whole time she was away. Poppycock! Livin' with a man, mark my words. Either she got rid of him or he of her. My valet, Purvis, will find out which in due time. Just like a ferret, that man. Never misses anything. What's Horatia Manners' re-appearance got to do with you anyway?"

The colour seeped into Topaz's cheeks and Lovat raised his eyebrows.

"Well, well. The godly Miss Chilcott, the ministering angel of Yelton, is in love with the Marquis of Rossmayne, is that it?"

She nodded, trying to avoid his eyes.

"And what about Manners? Does he feel the same?"

"Yes, but we aren't lovers. That is, we've never made love properly. We have met and held each other and we've kissed, but that's all."

Oswin let out a huge guffaw.

"I admire the man. Two wives and a mistress who isn't really a mistress, but would like to be one, if I'm not mistaken."

"Don't! This isn't funny. And there's so much more involved."

Lovat sobered.

"Do as I said. Start at the beginning."

Suddenly the flood-gates opened and Topaz let everything spill out from the day when she took Andrew's horse to the moment when Amsterdam asked her to marry him. She even spoke of Honor West's misery and her own guilt because she had let Mother Benedicta down.

When at last her voice trailed away, Lovat said musingly:

"There's a nice old muddle for you and I thought the Moor was a quiet place. That's why I built this house here thirty years ago. There's a bubbling cauldron under the surface and you wouldn't get a spicier intrigue in London at the height of the season than we've got down here. Well, what are you going to do about it?"

"I've thought and thought and in the end I decided I'd have to leave. Perhaps I'll go to another convent and test my vocation."

Lovat roared with laughter again.

"You'll never make a nun, you baggage. I know what's under that pious face you're wearing now. I said your name was pagan, and so are you."

She was defensive.

"I believe in God."

"So do I, strangely enough, but I'm not a monk. I've had a good few warming-pans in my bed over the years. No, a nunnery isn't the place for you. I've got a better idea."

"What sort of idea?"

"Nothing to frighten you, so don't look like that. I'm not long for this world and I might as well enjoy what time is left to me. Besides, I like meddling in other people's affairs; always have done. Marry me and I'll make you a fine lady and leave you a rich widow. That'll make both your beaux sit up and take notice."

She flushed scarlet.

"No! I couldn't – I – "

Oswin grinned.

"Don't be a dolt. I can't be a proper husband to you. Couldn't get the damned thing erect long enough."

"My lord!"

"And don't play the innocent with me. You know what I'm talking about, even if you and Manners haven't rolled in the hay. Use your head. You can't have Rossmayne and you don't want Amsterdam. Have me instead. You've nothing to lose and everything to gain, and I won't make you cry."

Topaz was in a daze. She had expected to get good advice from Lovat, not a proposal of marriage. Despite the shock she had received, she could see that what Oswin said made some kind of sense. But she had to give some thought to him, too. She couldn't use a good friend simply to get herself out of trouble.

"But you aren't in love with me."

For a second Lord Lovat said nothing and his eyes were veiled. Then he was merry again.

"All the better for you, but I care about you."

"Truly?"

"Most truly."

"But I would be taking advantage of your kindness and feelings for me."

"All women take advantage of the men in their lives if they get half a chance."

"I don't want to be like other women and cheat you. I must have time to think about this."

"I'll give you until you come next week; then I'll want your answer. And remember this. Andrew Manners may be exciting, but he's a rough sea: I am a safe harbour."

Topaz thought about that for a while. Then she rose and bent to touch Oswin's cheek with her lips.

"So you are, and perhaps you're right, my lord. Maybe it is time that I came in out of the storm."

* * *

After five days of torture and uncertainty, Topaz decided to accept Lovat's offer. As Oswin had said, she couldn't have Andrew and she didn't want Timothy. Furthermore, she was reaching the point when she knew she couldn't go on working with Beatrice and the others, deceiving them with her wrong-doings.

It was the day she made up her mind that she met Andrew on the Moor. She had yearned for a glimpse of him, and had wanted to tell him about Lovat herself, to make sure that he understood her reasons.

She expressed her regret at Virginia's death, feeling awkward.

"I'm so sorry. Timothy told me about it, and the return of Lady Horatia."

The marquis's mouth was a straight line.

"My only consolation is that for the first time in her life Horatia is in pain. She's brought it down on enough people's heads in the past. Now she's suffering, too."

"You think she really loved that man – Leinster?"

"Yes, I'm certain of it. She wasn't lying when she told me about him and she lies awake at night crying for him. I hope she goes on crying until the time comes for them to wrap a shroud round her."

"Andrew!"

"Well, how did you expect me to feel?"

Topaz sighed.

"As you do, I suppose, but I don't like to hear such bitterness in your voice. And I've got something to tell you which may make you feel the same way about me."

He looked at her quickly.

"I could never feel about you as I do about Horatia. What is your news?"

He listened silently, simply nodding when she had finished. He could never marry her and he had no right to stand in the way of any happiness she could find. At least she would be safe with Lovat and that knowledge gave him some comfort.

"It's not just because of us and because I can't go on tricking the Sisters. This must be our secret, but Timothy has asked me to marry him, too. I can't agree. He's too dear to me for me to pretend a love I don't feel."

The marquis was shaken.

"Timothy? I had no idea he felt like that. I told you once

before that I was selfish. I was too busy thinking about myself, and how I loved you, to notice what he was feeling. Is your mind really made up about Lovat?"

"Absolutely."

He looked at her sombrely.

"I wish things had been different so that we could have made love just once. I think I could bear losing you a little better if you had belonged to me, even for a short while."

Topaz could have expressed some brief regret, or simply shrugged in helplessness, but she didn't. She wanted Andrew and she said so plainly and without pretence.

"I feel the same. I want to be yours more than anything else in the world, and it's not too late.

"He will be my husband in name only and he knows I'm in love with you. He's very broadminded." She looked round the bleak Moor which offered no shelter to lovers or anyone else. "But there's nowhere for us to go, is there, Andrew?"

He smiled.

"Only the house which I bought when I suggested you should leave the Community. It's about a mile away. Come and see what you think of it."

Topaz inspected the stone cottage whilst the marquis lit a fire. Everything was in perfect order, as if the place was waiting patiently for its occupants to arrive. Logs in the grate, tinder box on the hearth. A soft bed, candles, and even bottles of wine and crystal glasses.

"It's perfect, and there isn't a speck of dust anywhere. You knew I'd come here one day, didn't you?"

"I prayed you would, and it's been cleaned regularly. Let's go and light a fire upstairs, too."

The bedroom was dim, full of mist seeping through the windows and the candles spluttered and wavered in the draught. Neither Andrew nor Topaz were aware of the gloom. They only saw each other.

As soon as Andrew began to undress her, Topaz felt an excitement she had never known before. It stirred something deep and primitive in her and she closed her eyes in bliss as the last garment dropped to the floor.

She lay relaxed on the bed, waiting for him, an odd, tingling sensation running through her. She had always wanted to feel his body against her own and now her wish was being granted. Flesh against flesh, just giving comfort and pleasure at first.

The marquis was a sophisticated and generous lover, well-versed in the art of pleasing women. Soon his hands started to run over her, caressing the fullness of her breasts, her nipples growing taut and straining against his palm as her back arched.

He moved down with sure, erotic touch to stroke the softness of her inner thighs and she stirred under him, her breath beginning to quicken.

When the calmness of the foreplay was over, they were honest in their desire. Topaz had never been with a man before, but some instinct told her how to arouse Andrew. She explored the place where his manhood lay and he, in turn, used experienced fingers to set alight that part of her where carnal longings had been damped down until that moment.

She began to writhe as they drew closer still, gasping and moaning as her hips matched the rhythm of his demands. She was no longer the dedicated, self-possessed Miss Chilcott of Yelton. She was a wild, tempestuous gypsy as their legs entwined and they rolled across the bed, first one on top, then the other, their open mouths meeting rapaciously.

Every sinew and muscle was engaged in the desperate fight to reach that ultimate peak of ecstasy when the mind blurs and the senses reel in the gratification of perfect sexual fulfilment. It could not be hurried, nor, when the time came, could it be held back. It mounted in voluptuous harmony, second by second. Topaz clawed Andrew's back, silently begging him to satisfy the ravenous craving within her which was reaching unbearable proportions. He responded with equal fervour, waiting until he was certain that she had reached her climax. Then he forced her legs apart, brutal in his final mastery.

She cried aloud in joyous elation, her body still on fire, holding on to the magical moment as long as she could.

Exhausted they lay side by side watching the flames dance on the ceiling.

"Oswin said I wasn't cut out to be a nun. He was right. No nun should feel as I do now. It was so wonderful and I wanted it to go on forever. Andrew, we could meet now and then. I could make some excuse and come here –"

He was gentle but definite.

"No, my darling, this has to be the end for us. A casual meeting whilst out walking on the Moor, even in your hidden places, is one thing. We've been fortunate that no one has seen us. This would be something quite different and our luck would very soon run out. Marry Lovat and be happy."

She propped herself up on one elbow.

"I suppose you're right. Miracles don't last for long, do they? But I am yours now, aren't I? Truly yours?"

"Yes, you're mine." He turned to look at her, marvelling at the perfection of her body and the animal passion he had found in her. "You'll always be mine, wherever you go and whatever you do."

There were tears on her cheeks. For a while she had been in paradise; now it was over. He saw her sorrow and wanted to weep, too, but men were forbidden such luxuries.

"Don't spoil it," he whispered. "I don't want to remember you like this."

"Then hold me again, tightly, tightly! If this is all we are ever to have of each other, let's use every second given to us. This has to last for the rest of our lives."

He pulled her down against him, feeling her eagerness and longing as their lips met again. The logs had lost their warmth, turning to grey ash; the candles burnt low and flickered out, but they didn't notice. They were together and they were in love.

For them, the world no longer existed.

* * *

When Topaz gave Lovat his answer she also told him the truth about her interlude with Andrew.

He wasn't angry or even surprised.

"As a matter of interest, where did you commit this adultery?"

She sighed.

"Yes, I suppose for Andrew it was adultery. He had bought a small house – a cottage really. He wanted me to leave the Order earlier, but I said I had to go on helping. It was the first time, my lord, and it will be the last."

Oswin was watching her with expressionless eyes.

"Enjoy it, did you?"

"It was wonderful, but terrible, too, because I'll never be with him again. I won't stop loving him; you know that, don't you?"

"Yes, you've made that plain enough and it doesn't bother me." It wasn't quite true, and Oswin found himself envying Rossmayne his youth and strength. "If you had any sense you'd forget him, but eat your heart out if you want to. Well, so you've decided to accept my offer, have you?"

"Yes, as long as you know the truth, and now I've told it."

He grunted.

"We'll leave for London in the morning. I've got a cranky female cousin, rich as Croesus, and well-born to boot. She's one of the gorgons who guard the doors of Almack's, so you'll be accepted everywhere you go."

"What's Almack's?"

"A ridiculous club run by exclusives for exclusives. You'll soon find out. Angela – my cousin is Lady Angela Hardwicke, by the way – will teach you all you need to know to enter society. You'll live with her until the wedding. We'll have a quiet one, no fuss. Can't abide fuss."

"I'd like it to be quiet as well, but I'm beginning to feel nervous. I have no idea how to behave in the *beau monde* – is that the right phrase?"

"It'll do and that's what Angela will teach you."

Topaz looked uncomfortable.

"I hate to mention this, because it seems as though I'm asking for things, but you do know I haven't got anything to wear, don't you? I mean, I've got this dress and another like it, but that's all."

Oswin waved her worries aside.

"By the time Angela's finished spending my money you won't be able to get into your room for gowns, cloaks, shoes and other falderols."

"You mustn't let her spend too much on me." Topaz made an instant protest. "I don't want to bankrupt you."

"You won't. Not even Angela could do that. I lack a good many things, but money ain't one of 'em. Here, I've got something for you."

Topaz stared at the ring with the huge ruby surrounded by diamonds, her eyes like saucers.

"Take it. It belonged to my grandmother. She'd have liked you."

"I don't know what to say." Gingerly, Topaz slipped the ring on one finger, her voice hushed. "It's very, very beautiful."

Lovat was pleased at her reaction and leaned forward to pat her hand.

"And so are you, Topaz Chilcott," he said with a grin. "By God, so are you."

Seven

By the time the season began, Topaz was more than ready to take her place in society.

Lady Angela Hardwicke, an elderly and extremely eccentric female with ginger hair, had taken to her at once.

"Confound it, Lovat," she had said upon first setting eyes on Topaz. "How in God's Name did you snare a creature like this? I declare she'll outshine every woman in London and make you the envy of every man who meets her. As for you, my girl, what on earth do you see in this fat porpoise?"

Topaz was soon to learn that the colourful and derogatory remarks which passed between Angela and Oswin meant nothing, but at first she had been startled.

"Well, Lady Angela, I – "

"Suppose it's his money. Well, I can't say I blame you. Where are your trunks and boxes?"

"I haven't any." Topaz was short. "Apart from another gown like this, and a shift or two, I've got nothing. And, madam, be assured. I'm not marrying Lord Lovat for his money."

Angela cackled.

"A firebrand. I like that."

"There's something else you ought to know."

"No need to go into that," Lovat mumbled. "No one's business but your own."

"Be quiet, Oswin." Lady Angela was agog. "What ought I to know? You're a Russian princess in disguise? Or a – "

"I'm illegitimate and my mother was a Romany."

"Splendid!"

Topaz was taken aback.

"You don't mind? I understood that high birth was all important in your circles."

"Only if you're trying to catch a duke and your mother was a washerwoman, your father a baker. You've already got Oswin, so it doesn't really matter much. However, I think it's something we'll keep to ourselves, at least for the time being."

There followed an orgy of shopping as Lovat had predicted. Topaz was pulled first one way then the other by dressmakers. Bales of material of every type and hue were spread before her for her approval. Boxes of shoes and boots filled the corners of the room. Reticules, gloves, parasols covered the bed. A maid, Nancy Brown, was appointed to wait on her and hairdressers hovered over her cooing their praises.

Topaz didn't have to worry about making choices, for Angela did that for her. Even the jewels which Lovat bought as gifts were scrutinised carefully by the fierce mentor, to make sure that they were adequate and sufficiently costly.

The manners which Topaz had been taught at the convent were good enough as a basis for acceptable behaviour, but she soon discovered that she had a great deal more to learn, and would also have to adopt a whole new set of values. She didn't like many of them, but she didn't want Oswin to be ashamed of her and Angela gave her scant chance to protest.

At her first ball she wore a plain, high-bodiced gown of lemon-coloured silk, with slippers to match. Her hair had been swept up to the top of her head, from whence it was allowed to fall in ringlets to her neck. She had the simplest of gold chains round her throat, for Angela knew what she was doing.

"Any woman can get herself stared at if she's loaded down with diamonds and other gewgaws. You don't need 'em, child. You wait and see."

A stunned silence greeted her appearance, every eye turned to watch the progress of the girl who looked like a goddess. She was a sensation, the talk of the evening, and Angela was well-satisfied.

"That's a good start," she said. "Now remember. Be cool and distant and you'll have every man at your feet and every woman ready to tear your eyes out."

Topaz found it very difficult to obey the command for constant disdain, and soon shed it for a charm which worked like magic. There were a few females who were hostile, but most liked her. The men were bowled over, and Topaz received many gifts of flowers, sweetmeats, and other trifles and a shower of love poems which she read aloud to

Oswin as they rocked with laughter.

When she wasn't shopping, making or receiving calls, or at the dressmakers, Topaz went riding during the day accompanied by Angela and Oswin. She loved Hyde Park because it was the nearest thing she'd seen to the countryside since she had arrived in the capital. The grass was green, deer ran gracefully between the trees, cows munched unhurriedly beside the many streams.

The patronesses of Almack's, Lady Castlereagh, Lady Jersey, Lady Cowper, Lady Sefton, Mrs. Drummond Burrell, Princess Esterhazy and the Countess Lieven, accepted her entry into the holy of holies without question. She was Lady Hardwicke's protegée, and Lady Hardwicke was one of the *grandes dames* who made the rules of that remarkable establishment.

Topaz thought Almack's rather dull after some of the splendid places she had visited. Its décor was modest, its weekly ball, held every Wednesday, provided the minimum of refreshment, such as weak bohea, lemonade, thinly-cut bread and butter and not very fresh cake.

One could only enter this sacred temple to snobbishness if one had a voucher of admission and they were harder to obtain than the stars out of the sky. Birth, riches and fame were no guarantee of a ticket. One had to have *ton,* and it was the patronesses who decided who had it and who did not.

Beau Brummel had laid down the requirements for men's evening wear at Almack's. Dark coat, usually blue, perfectly tailored; white waistcoat and stiff white cravat. Some still wore knee breeches, but tightly-fitting pantaloons buttoned round the ankle over white silk socks were permitted. Shoes had to be low-heeled and black.

The women wore ball gowns and jewels and looked like royal butterflies.

In the evening between the hours of six and eight, and later from ten to midnight, the streets of the West End seemed to Topaz to become a fairyland. One magnificent carriage followed another, candles blazing in their ornate glass holders, footmen in powdered wigs and bright livery up behind. The noise of wheels on uneven roads mingled with the voices of the élite as they alighted at their respective destinations and made their slow and stately way into the houses which had lights in every room from attic to cellar.

No one did very much, Topaz noticed. There were no card games, no sound of music, nor food served. The famous and high-born simply moved from room to room, inclining their heads or smiling as they aknowledged their friends and acquaintances. When the milling crowd had snaked its way through each house, they all departed in a flurry of silks and satins, slamming coach doors, and the shouts of the footmen to the coachmen. Then they moved on and repeated the whole performances two streets away.

When asked by Topaz if the procedure was not a waste of time, Lady Angela had given a shocked squawk.

"Its *the* thing to be seen, my dear. One doesn't do, one is just there."

The high-light of Topaz's season came when she was introduced to the Prince Regent. He had graciously accepted an invitation to a drum at Lady Angela's luxurious house in Belgravia, nodding affably to Lovat as he acknowledged the bows and curtsies of his future subjects.

"Well, if it ain't Lovat. M'dear fellow, where have you sprung from? Thought you were in the West Country."

Oswin straightened up.

"So I was, sir, but I thought my bride had better see something of what's goin' on in town before I take her back and bury her on the Moor. Sir, may I present my wife, Topaz?"

Topaz gave a deep curtsey and found herself raised up by a royal hand.

"You've married this dull stick?" The Regent and Lovat had known each other for a long time and shared affection and respect. "'Pon my soul, I don't know what the world's comin' to. Room's full of Adonises and you've matched yourself with this rogue. Lovat, you're gettin' fatter."

Oswin leered.

"Only my deep devotion to you, sir, and a thought for my future acceptance at Court, prevents me from repaying the compliment."

The Regent gave a delighted laugh.

"Old reprobate. Here, bring this vision to Carlton House next week. A ball on Thursday. Be there, and that's a royal command."

And so Topaz went to Carlton House and, when the heat of summer came, she and Oswin went to Brighton, following the Regent's train to a mini-season at that most desirable resort.

Angela had no more worries about her charge. She had been accepted everywhere, approved by the Prince and, even more importantly, by Brummell.

"You're made, my girl," she said complacently. "I hope Lovat's pleased."

"Ma'm, do you think Oswin is all right? He looks a bad colour to me."

Angela shot a glance to the other side of the room where her cousin was dozing.

"Bit less to say for himself than usual, but that's no bad thing."

"It's more than that. He seems so tired."

"No stamina, that's his trouble. Don't bother your pretty head about him, m'dear. He'll do well enough."

But twelve months after they had married with such discretion, Lovat announced that he wanted to return home.

"Out of sorts, d'yer see, m'dear?" He had gone to bed early, not even wanting his supper. "Would you mind that much?"

"Of course not." Topaz sat beside him and held his hand. "I know you're not feeling well. I've seen that for some time. We've had a marvellous year. I've met everybody and done everything. I'd like to go home, too."

She tried not to think about Andrew, but Oswin knew what was passing through her mind.

"Rossmayne'll still be there. That bother you?"

"No. We're bound to meet, of course, but he's very civilised. After twelve months with Lady Angela, so am I."

"Thank God she didn't spoil you. I was afraid at first she might turn you into one of these ridiculous society cats who insist on seeing a man's family tree before speaking to him. But she hasn't done that."

"I owe her a great deal. I couldn't have done any of the things I did without her."

"Yes, she turned up trumps, I'll say that for her."

"When shall we go?"

"Don't want to interfere with any special engagements you've got. A week or two, maybe?"

Topaz's hand tightened.

"We'll go to-morrow morning. Will Angela be able to let this house for us?"

"She could, but I thought we'd keep it. Never know; we might come back one day."

"Whatever you say."

Lovat wiped perspiration from his brow, feeling his heart thudding uncomfortably.

"You're a good child. Now, off you go and give me some peace. Go with Angela and buy a new hat."

"Sir, I've got dozens of new hats."

"Buy a dozen more, and Topaz – "

"Yes?"

"Thank you for marryin' me. Much obliged, my girl; very much obliged to you, and that's a fact."

* * *

As soon as Topaz returned to Stone Towers she set about its renovation. It was still as gloomy as the day on which she had first seen it and she longed to transform it into a place of splendid elegance.

"Striped walls in the dining-room, Oswin; pale green, I think. We'll have to have a new carpet and different chairs and table. Now, in the drawing-room – "

Lovat listened with affectionate amusement.

"Do what you like, so long as you leave my bedroom alone. Lived with clutter for thirty years; I intend to die with it, too."

"Don't say that!"

"What? Clutter?"

"No, you know what I mean."

"Everyone dies in the end. It's just a matter of when and how. But just because I promised I'd make you a rich widow, don't think you're going to get rid of me yet. I'll be right as rain now we're home. London never did suit me. Everyone always dashin' about like lunatics. Don't know how George stands it."

"George?"

"The Regent. We go back a long way, he and I."

"I guessed that. He really was pleased to see you; it wasn't just politeness."

"No, and I was glad to see him, even though he did say I was gettin' fatter. Damned impertinence."

"Royal prerogative."

"Don't side with him, you vixen. Go and buy some curtains or whatever it is you want."

Now and then, Topaz emerged from the supervision of the workmen and seamstresses to go riding on the Moor. She wanted to see Timothy to explain personally why she had married Oswin. She couldn't call on him at home. It would embarrass him and she wasn't sure that Lady Agatha would receive her. So she kept her eyes open for him, hoping for a chance meeting.

The morning she saw him she suddenly felt butterflies in her stomach. She had rehearsed her speech so many times and had been mightily cool and controlled about it all. Now her self-confidence fled as he raised his hat, gazing at her as if she were a total stranger.

"I'm glad to see you, Timothy. I've been looking out for you."

He didn't make things easy for her because her marriage had hurt him badly. He had understood her feelings for Andrew; he couldn't comprehend her reasons for marrying Lovat.

"I'm flattered, my lady."

She coloured.

"I can't get used to being called that."

"I'm sure you will. You are most adaptable."

It was a question of whether to turn away with tears in her eyes, admitting failure, or giving Amsterdam a taste of her temper. She chose the latter and alighted from her carriage as Timothy began to move away.

"Don't you dare walk off when I'm talking to you, Timothy Amsterdam. If you think I've forgotten how to rough a man up, I can assure you I haven't. You stand still and listen to what I've got to say, and if you don't stop looking at me like that I'll hit you over the head with this."

She brandished her reticule fiercely and Amsterdam was halted in his tracks. He watched in awe as she wrenched off her smart hat and threw it into the carriage with her gloves.

"That's better," she said, her eyes ablaze. "You think I married Oswin Lovat for his name and his money, I suppose?"

"Your reason for marrying Lord Lovat is none – "

"Shut up! I haven't finished. He knows, as you do, that I'm in love with Andrew. I also told him of my affection for you and that I couldn't injure you by marrying you without love. Can't you see what it would be like, you blind, stupid man? Every time we kissed, you'd know I was kissing Andrew in my heart. Each time we went to bed, you'd realize that it was Andrew I wanted to lay with. I wouldn't do that to you, Timothy. I care about you far too much. I couldn't stay with the Sisters because of Andrew; it would be betraying their trust. Andrew can never be mine and, as I've just said, I couldn't hurt you. I told Oswin all of this and he proposed marriage. We've never lived as husband and wife and never will. He's a dear, kind man who said he was a safe harbour for me, and he's been just that."

"Topaz – "

"Will you stop interrupting and pay heed to me? I didn't have to pretend with Oswin; I still don't. He knows what fondness I have for him, but he's got no illusions about whom I really want. It doesn't matter to him. I didn't want his title or his money, although I must say in all honesty I did enjoy the London season. The clothes his cousin, Lady Angela, chose for me were quite the most fabulous things you've ever seen." She paused, raising her reticule again. "Why are you laughing?"

"Because you are the most divine creature I have ever known. I thought so on the day you stole Andrew's horse; I still think so. And you're right; I'm a fool. It wouldn't have worked for us. I told myself I could live with the thought of having just a small part of your life and love, but when you put it into words a few moments ago I could see how awful it would have been. I might have ended up hating you."

"Worse. You might have started to hate Andrew."

"That, too, perhaps. When I heard about your marriage I felt so useless and rejected. People in love are peculiar that way, you know. Forgive me and do put that thing down. You're making me quite nervous."

Topaz went into Timothy's arms as quietly and naturally as if nothing had happened. He accepted her kiss for what it was, and was curiously soothed by it. There was more than one kind of love and he was lucky to have even a small share of hers.

They talked for a while about London and about the alterations which Topaz was making at Stone Towers. Then she said casually:

"And how is Andrew?"

Amsterdam's smile faded.

"Not as he was. Horatia leads him a dog's life. She is a nagging shrew."

"Why does he let her do it to him?"

"For the sake of peace, I suppose, and the children."

Topaz saw his face darken.

"Timothy? What is it? Is something wrong with Curtis or Rodney?"

"Curtis is perfectly all right, but Rodney isn't. Horatia, Connell and the girl whom Horatia has employed as a nursemaid, are ill-treating the boy and that is unforgivable."

"Ill-treating him? But surely Andrew wouldn't let them."

"He doesn't know. He spends as much time out of the house as possible, and what they do is too subtle for him to notice. I wouldn't have known myself, but I happen to have a pair of ears in that establishment. I'm told the nursemaid takes the child's food away from him after he's taken only a bite or so. He's never given enough clean clothes and he's chastized for the slightest thing. But they're careful not to hit him where the bruises will shew. Topaz?"

Topaz had turned very pale, her eyes filled with such fury that Amsterdam recoiled.

"I won't let this happen," she said softly, not even aware that Timothy was still there. "Rodney is Andrew's son and I'm going to stop it."

"But you can't go charging into High Brook making wild accusations. Even I haven't got any proof yet; only a servant's word. But if things get any worse, I'll talk to Andrew. Topaz, please don't – "

"Things won't have a chance to get worse and don't worry. I'm not that silly. I shan't take on the marchioness without the right weapons."

"But where will you get them from?"

"I don't know yet, but I'll find them."

"My dear, I can see how much this has upset you. Perhaps I shouldn't have told you."

Topaz met his worried eyes again.

"Yes you should. You ought to have told me as soon as

you knew what was happening. I am a titled lady who danced with the Regent at Carlton House, but remember this. First, I was a gypsy and gypsies never forget and they never forgive. I hated what Horatia Manners did to Andrew and Virginia. I hate what she is doing to Rodney even more.

"He is Andrew's son and I'm going to protect him no matter what it takes. Now get out of my way, Timothy. I've got work to do."

* * *

Lovat listened to Topaz, torn between anger directed against Horatia Manners, and admiration for his wife's loveliness which was always at its best when she was in a rage. And she was in a fine old rage now.

Somehow the pins in her hair always seemed to escape when she lost her temper and the dark tresses whirled round her shoulders as she walked up and down Oswin's bedroom.

"I would like to kill her," she said finally. "I would like to put my hands round her throat and squeeze until she stopped breathing."

"I expect Manners 'ud like to do the same."

"He should have done so a long time ago. Then Rodney wouldn't be tormented like this. Oswin, he doesn't get enough to eat."

Lovat looked at the tears rolling down Topaz's cheeks and held out his hands.

"Come here, m'dear. Don't like to see you upset like this. Better do something about it, hadn't we?"

"Timothy says I can't just storm into High Brook and he's right. I was full of threats and said I'd get the right weapons to fight the marchioness, but it was a bluff. Where can I possibly get them from?"

"From me, my girl, from me. How would you like to have young Rodney livin' here with us?"

It was as if the sun had suddenly come out and for all his

age and infirmity, Lovat caught his breath. Topaz's smile dazzled him, her eyes threatened to drown him. He quickly brought himself back to earth before she gave him another dizzy spell.

"There's nothing in the world I'd like more. It would be like having part of Andrew with me always. Oh, my dear, I'm sorry. I didn't mean – "

"Don't be a fool, woman. I know you're still in love with Rossmayne."

"But the marchioness will never let us have him. She's punishing Andrew for marrying Virginia, even though it was her own fault that he did so."

"As I understand it from Purvis, Madam Marchioness is wallowing in despair because she loved a man who chucked her out. I knew Purvis would get to the bottom of it in time. Man must have been a damned sensible fellow to get rid of Horatia Manners. But she'll hit back at anyone around her, just because of what's happened to her. Gettin' unstable, I shouldn't wonder."

Topaz was dubious. Oswin had been right about his valet. There was very little going on in the neighbourhood, or even further afield, of which Purvis was not apprised.

"I'm sure you're right," she said. "But how does that help us? Are we to blackmail her because of her lost lover? There wouldn't be much point. Andrew knows about him."

Lovat smiled satanically.

"We're going to blackmail her, but not because of the lucky devil who got away. You see, Horatia has had other lovers. Usually she is careful, at least whilst she's down here, but once she and one of her beaux tripped up. They came out of a summer house or folly, or some such thing, and found themselves in the company of a servant girl who was out walking. She'd wandered a bit, I suppose. Girls do wander."

"Oswin! Go on. What happened?"

Lord Lovat's face was no longer amused and his eyes were cold, like chips of ice.

"They grabbed her and threatened her. Then the man began to beat her, but he hit her too hard. Purvis saw it all and followed the wretched pair to where they buried the body.

"Everyone assumed the girl had run away. Servants often run off if they don't like their mistress, or fall out with the rest of the staff. Anyway, no one thought anything of it at the time."

"And you didn't tell Andrew?"

"Don't look so shocked. No, I didn't tell him and I warned Purvis to keep quiet about it, too. I like Rossmayne and I didn't want him mixed up in a scandal. Murder tends to be a scandalous affair, don't you see? Wouldn't have brought the wench back, so there seemed no point in turning his world upside down. Don't you tell him either, because he'd feel honour bound to do something about it. He hasn't got a pliable conscience like me."

"What if he asks me a direct question?"

"Lie," returned Oswin promptly, "and do it with conviction. Tell him it's the sort of thing no woman would want let out of the bag. Then smile at him and he'll forget to ask anything else."

"I hope you're right."

"I know I am. Go and visit the marchioness to-morrow and tell her the story. Say my valet is alive and well and has an excellent memory. Ask her if she can remember where the body was hidden. Probably only bones now, poor thing, but that, together with Purvis's testimony, will be enough. If the location has slipped her mind, my man will be only too happy to remind her."

"But the authorities will want to know why Purvis didn't report the killing."

"This won't get to the ears of the authorities, my treasure; Horatia will make sure of that. I think you'll find she'll hand Rodney over readily enough. Hanging's a nasty business."

Topaz put her arms round Oswin and hugged him.

"You are wonderful," she said and meant it. "Who could ask for a better weapon than that? Dearest Oswin, you are so clever."

"Yes, I am rather, aren't I?" he replied complacently. "Now, how about a drop of that forbidden brandy as a reward?"

Eight

On her way to High Brook, Topaz met Andrew. It was the first time she had seen him since they had been together in the cottage which they had left full of their memories to be.

It was cool for a July morning and Topaz wore a riding dress of soft green, trimmed with braid on the bodice and cuffs in military style. The small beaver hat was worn at a fashionable tilt, flaunting a long green ostrich feather stitched across the front brim. The ensemble was completed by black half-boots, green fringed; York tan gloves, and a silver-topped riding whip.

They dismounted and walked the few yards which separated them, Andrew hardly able to believe his eyes. He had seen her in rags, in a plain uniform of the convent, but never dressed *à la mode,* and the sight stunned him.

"Have I changed so much?"

He stopped staring, trying to suppress the instinctive desire to catch hold of her.

"No, at least I don't think so. It's the fine feathers which have reduced me to silence."

"Will I do?"

"You will do very well. My, dear, it's good to see you again."

"The months have dragged."

"Even in London? Word has come to me that you created something of a sensation."

"I suppose I should say something blasé to that, such as: 'Là, sir, you flatter me. After all, what is so extraordinary about dining at Carlton House?' But I'm not going to pretend I didn't enjoy it, even though I missed you so much."

"How is Lovat? I gather he wasn't well."

"He's better now he's home. Andrew, I have to talk to you. It's important."

"Everything you say to me is important."

"This is about Rodney."

He frowned.

"Rodney? I don't understand."

"He is in a most unfortunate situation."

"I think you'd better explain." Rossmayne was no longer smiling. "You seem to know more about my son than I do. Speak simply, if you please."

The marquis was white round the mouth by the time Topaz had finished.

"And the source of your information?"

"That I cannot divulge, but I hope you will believe me when I say that it is a good and reliable one."

"I'll kill her." Rossmayne struck his riding boot with his crop. "Horatia is doing this to hit back at me because I insisted on Rodney remaining in my house. I haven't spent enough time there to ensure that he was all right. I have failed him, and Virginia. I said I would give him everything including love and I have broken my promise. I'm obliged to you. Now if you'll excuse me I have a reckoning to make with my wife."

"Wait." Topaz put out a restraining hand. "Hear me out, because I haven't finished. The marchioness isn't worth killing. I'll take the boy away from her. Would you let him come and live with Oswin and me?"

She watched the fury drain from his face and when he spoke it was with gentleness.

"There is nothing I would like better. It would be as if he were our child. But Horatia won't just hand him over because you ask her to. She'll want to go on ill-treating him to pay me out. I'll have to bring him to you myself."

"No. If that way were chosen, no matter how carefully we guarded Rodney, someone could get at him."

"But I don't see – "

"If we do it my way, she will never dare to harm him again."

"But simply asking her to – "

Topaz's smile was brief and without humour.

"I'm not going to ask her, my lord, I'm going to tell her. You see, there is something which Oswin's valet knows about your wife which she will most certainly not want voiced abroad. It's his secret, so I can't give you details, but be assured – it will be effective."

"You are full of secrets this morning."

"Yes, I'm sorry but they are not really mine to share. Will you trust me?"

"This information Lovat's man has; is it something to do with Horatia's disappearance and return?"

"No, nothing. It was an incident earlier in her life. You haven't answered my question."

The marquis took a deep breath.

"Yes, I'll trust you, but if you fail, I'll remove Rodney from High Brook myself."

"Very well, but I shan't fail."

"What about Lovat? Are you sure he is agreeable to the idea? It's asking a lot of a man to take in another's child, especially if – "

" – he knows his wife is in love with the boy's father?" Topaz laid a hand on Andrew's arm, reassuring him. "It was his idea. He is a very special man and I am privileged to know him."

Andrew's fingers closed over hers.

"He is privileged, too. Do you ever think of our cottage?"

"Constantly. It is always in my thoughts and dreams. I

shall never forget it."

"Nor I. Sometimes I'm afraid I may have made things worse for you by taking you there."

"How can you be so foolish? I had a glimpse of heaven; not many people have such a prop with which to go through life."

"I miss you. God, Topaz, I miss you so much."

Moisture hung on her dark lashes making her eyes more brilliant still.

"And I you, dearest. If I could have one kiss – "

"No, it's too risky. Someone may be watching us. I told you before our luck wouldn't last for ever. Besides, if I were to take you in my arms now it wouldn't end with a kiss. I would rip that fine green habit from your back and pull you down to this rough earth and make love to you.

"I want to feel your soft skin under my hands as I did before, your mouth against mine. I want to caress you and sense your excitement grow until it fans my own desire to white heat. I want the surrender of your body to mine as I possess you, and to hear the cry which tells me I have not failed you.

"Damn it, Topaz, go away before it's too late."

"I'll go," she whispered. "We mustn't start a scandal at this of all times. For Rodney's sake I'll ride on, but I want you, Andrew. Oh, my darling, I want you!"

Then she was up in the saddle again, all grace and swift movement as she raced past him to Grimspound. He looked round carefully but there was no one about, so he took a kerchief from his pocket, quickly brushing away his own tears, shed for a woman he would love for all his days, but who would never be his again.

* * *

Topaz had learned a great deal from Lovat and even more from Lady Angela. She didn't waste time apologizing for her unexpected appearance at High Brook. She simply walked past Denning, demanding to know where the drawing-room was and ordering the startled butler to fetch his mistress.

"I am Lady Lovat," she said shortly. "Tell the marchioness to make haste for I am busy."

Horatia stormed into the room. She had grown plumper in her discontent and she was bulging somewhat precariously from the high-waisted dress with an extremely low *décolletage*.

Food was not her only consolation. Nettie Connell alone knew how much she drank, and although it was early in the day there was already the odour of liquor on her breath.

"How dare you come here?" Her colour was high, her eyes glittering. "I know all about you."

For one dreadful moment Topaz thought the marchioness had discovered her liaison with Rossmayne, but her expression didn't change.

"Oh?"

"Yes, you're that tinker who managed to hook Oswin Lovat and what an imbecile he must be."

"There is not a drop of tinker's blood in me, you damned woman."

Horatia was jolted. She had expected her unwelcome visitor to cringe, for no one of lowly origins like to be reminded of the fact. But the girl in the smart green habit, with a face like a madonna, hadn't batted an eyelash.

"Well, what do you want? And whatever it is, you should have gone to the servants' entrance."

"The Lovats come and go through the front door, madam. As to what I want. I'm taking Rodney home with me. He is to live with Oswin and me. His father is in total agreement."

The marchioness shrieked with pure rage.

"You want what, you whore?"

"I want that child whom you and some of your servants are mistreating."

Horatia paused. Someone had been talking and whoever

it was would learn to rue the day they were born. Meanwhile she had to get rid of the upstart whose steady gaze met her own.

"What's the bastard to do with you? Whatever rumours you've heard are lies. The boy is perfectly happy here."

"Rodney is not fed properly, nor kept clean. And those who are beaten for no particular reason are seldom happy."

Horatia stopped bothering with protestations.

"You seem more concerned about him than his father is, but there's nothing you can do about it. I'm keeping Rodney here so that I can rub Manners' nose in his illegitimacy. Andrew won't take him away from me."

"He might go with him."

"And leave High Brook and his heir? He'd never do that."

"You may be right, but we're not discussing what the marquis might or might not do. It's what you're going to do. You're going to give me the child."

"And if I don't? What then, you impudent trollop?"

"Then I shall go and fetch my husband's valet and a constable."

Horatia didn't see the trap.

"A constable has no authority over me. And your husband's valet! What are you talking about? Are you feeble-witted?"

"No. As to what Purvis could do, he could explain where you and one of your lovers hid the body of a servant girl you killed a few years ago. Purvis saw the whole thing, you see.

"Lovat made him keep quiet at the time because he didn't want the marquis involved in the scandal of a homicide. But that time is past and Purvis has an excellent memory. He knows where your lover dug the hole. I don't suppose there's much of the poor girl left, but there will be some remains and Purvis is renowned for his probity. He will swear an oath and that'll be good enough."

The marchioness's colour had faded. She had almost forgotten that night; it had been so long ago. Now she could recall vividly how she and Charles Beckwith had emerged from an old summer house, their clothing rumpled, both still aroused from their love-making. She could see the maid standing there, eyes wide.

Charles had lost his head because he had drunk too much wine. When the girl had started to run he had chased her, dragging her back and hitting her over and over again. Horatia could remember how she had cried out to him to stop, but he had paid no attention in his frenzy. Then it was over. She, the Marchioness of Rossmayne, was a party to a murder and she'd had to help Beckwith get rid of the body.

Nothing had happened. Beckwith had gone away and no one remarked on the servant's disappearance. After a month or so Horatia had breathed again and in a year the incident had passed from her mind. After all, the girl had only been a kitchenmaid or some such menial and of no importance.

She looked back at the implacable young woman who was still regarding her with contempt. A common gypsy in expensive clothes who could be her undoing. She didn't bother to deny the charges; there was little point. Topaz Lovat had got her facts right and clearly was prepared to use them with the aid of an eye-witness.

"But why you?" she said at last. "Why does Rossmayne want Rodney to live with you?"

"The marquis and Oswin are friends. We are childless and can give the boy everything he needs. It is an ideal arrangement."

Horatia looked for some hidden reason for the proposal, but couldn't read one in Topaz's eyes.

"If I agree, how do I know you'll keep silent? You, your husband and his valet?"

"Because I give you my word that we'll do so."

"The word of a tinker?"

"The promise of a Romany. I never break my promises. Neither does Lord Lovat."

Topaz gave Horatia a final look, knowing she had won. The marchioness seemed to have sagged, her anger gone. It was time to end it and Topaz said briskly:

"Well, madam, what is it to be? Will you send for Rodney, or shall I go and fetch Purvis and the authorities?"

* * *

Rodney was welcomed with open arms at Stone Towers. He was a thin little boy with blond hair and unhappy blue eyes. Topaz could see nothing of Andrew in him, guessing that he favoured his dead mother.

It didn't take long to put some flesh on his bones and laughter in his eyes. Everyone spoilt him from Topaz and Oswin down to the newest maid in the kitchen. He had more toys than he knew what to do with and clothes galore. One of the servants, Amy Parks who had nine brothers and sisters, was chosen to be his nursemaid. She was soft, easy-going and loved small children. In no time at all Rodney turned from a frightened shadow to a normal, mischievous boy.

One day when Rodney was with Oswin and Topaz he looked up from the carved wooden animals with which he was playing.

"I do like being with you," he said and gave Topaz a solemn look which brought a lump to her throat. "I won't have to go back to the marchioness, will I?"

"No, boy." Oswin blew his nose vigorously. "Never again. Your father will visit you as often as he can."

"I'm glad. It wasn't very nice at High Brook. I got so hungry, you see."

Lovat and Topaz exchanged a glance.

"That won't happen here."

"No, I don't suppose it will. Amy is always trying to make me take second helpings. Of course, I don't want to get fat. If I got fat I couldn't beat her when we have races."

Timothy was a regular caller. He had come to terms with Topaz's marriage and just seeing her made his life worth while.

"I don't suppose you'll tell me about the weapons you found, will you?" he asked one day as he and Topaz watched Rodney chase the unfortunate Amy in and out of the rose bushes. "Whatever they were, they were effective."

"No, I can't tell you." She smiled at Amsterdam in a way which made his longing for her almost unendurable. "I had help, of course. The main thing is that Rodney is now safe and he'll remain so."

"Andrew comes to see him?"

"Naturally."

"Hard for you."

Topaz turned and met Timothy's eyes.

"No harder than for you, my dear. We are a sad trio, aren't we?"

"I try hard not to be. After all, things might have worked out so that I never saw you again."

"Don't love me so much, Timothy."

"Don't love Andrew so much, Topaz."

They both laughed and their hands clasped in mutual comfort.

"I wonder how it will end," said Amsterdam. "I suppose your Aunt Liti could tell us."

Topaz's smile was gone.

"I don't want to know. I think that if we could see into the future we wouldn't have the courage to live the present."

"You're not a proper gypsy at all, but you're right. God didn't intend us to see ahead and I don't want to know the day on which I shall have to say good-bye to you."

"Nor I the hour which is the last that Andrew and I will share. Good gracious, how morbid we are becoming and it's time for tea. I'll go and see to that and you do something useful for a change, Mr. Amsterdam."

"I am at your bidding, Lady Lovat. What am I to do?"

"Bestir yourself and try to catch that young limb of Satan for me. It's high time poor Amy Parks had a rest."

* * *

Honor West was riding on the Moor when she met Amsterdam returning from the Lovats'.

She watched him approach with the same old melancholy. When she had heard that Topaz was to marry Lord Lovat her world had become a new and sunny place. Timothy couldn't marry his Romany now; she was beyond his reach.

Gradually, however, Honor realized that nothing much had changed and the grey clouds of despondency returned. Topaz wasn't Timothy's wife, of course, but he was still in love with her, still visiting her whenever he could, and hardly ever calling upon herself and Lady West.

"Honor. You're a long way from home."

She coloured furiously as he dismounted. She couldn't admit that she watched his comings and goings as often as her duties permitted and that many times she had followed him in the direction of Stone Towers.

"I missed my path," she said, realizing how weak her excuse must sound. "I suppose I was thinking of something else."

Amsterdam looked at her with pity. Once he had known how she felt about him he had tried to avoid her, having nothing to offer her but unhappiness. Now and then they encountered each other, but their conversation tended to be stilted, both so anxious to avoid the subject which had spoilt their childhood friendship.

"I'm glad I've seen you," he lied, trying to put a good face on things. "I'm going away for a while. An uncle of mine has died and I'm his executor."

"I see. You're going to London? That will be pleasant for you."

"Not very. I'm not a lover of the metropolis, but I expect I'll be too busy for it to bother me this time."

The word 'lover' made Honor flush again and for once she was quite glad when Amsterdam made his adieux and rode off.

Lady West always knew when her daughter had seen

Amsterdam. It was as if she were a witch, with an all-seeing eye focused on Honor and she never missed the opportunity of taunting the girl.

"And how was Mr. Amsterdam to-day?"

"I don't know what you mean."

"Don't be stupid, you know quite well what I mean. You saw him, didn't you? Your cheeks are crimson and very unbecoming. They never look like that unless you've met him. What a blockhead you are. He doesn't want you, can't you see that? Even now that gypsy's married he can't leave her be. Everyone knows how often he goes to see her."

"He goes to see Rodney, the marquis's son."

Lady West made a vulgar noise.

"Your capacity for deluding yourself is infinite. By the way, Mr. Chambers is dining with us next Tuesday. I've bought a piece of sprigged muslin so that you can have a new dress. Mrs. Luke will be coming to fit you to-morrow. Try to do something with your hair and for heaven's sake stop pouting. What will Mr. Chambers think of you?"

"I don't care what he thinks of me, mother."

"Well you should. He's been most patient and he's very interested in you; he told me so. That's more than Amsterdam will ever be."

Honor went to her room and looked in the mirror. Her mother was right about one thing; her hair was a mess. The droop of her mouth wasn't caused through pouting, but through a sense of utter defeat.

It was then that it struck her that Timothy's pain must be just as bad as her own. He loved Topaz, but could never have her. All he had to look forward to was the odd hour or two spent with her. She had been selfish in her suffering, never thinking of Timothy's anguish.

"I could help you," she said in another of her one-sided conversations with him. "I know I could. Even if you don't love me, I could be a companion to you so that you didn't feel alone.

"I wouldn't ask anything of you; just to be near to you

and give you comfort. I think I'll suggest it when you come back, but don't say no, Timothy. Oh, my dearest, please, please don't say no."

* * *

Lady Agatha and Fidelma had been racked with curiosity when Rodney Manners suddenly moved to Stone Towers. They plied Timothy with questions which he wouldn't answer.

"I can't discuss it with you, Aunt Ag," he'd said very firmly for him. "It's not my business, but I can assure you it's the best thing which could happen to the boy."

"Mr. Timothy's been to Stone Towers again today," said Fidelma as she was helping her mistress to dress. "Went there to say good-bye, likely as not, seeing he's on his way to London in a couple of days."

"I hope he'll go a good deal further than that," returned Agatha, holding a rope of matchless pearls against her ageing skin and pulling a face at the result. "My brother had a lot of interests in the West Indies. Best thing that could happen to the boy – travelling half across the world."

"Perhaps he'll meet someone nice on the boat."

"Ship, you ignoramus. And I think that's highly unlikely."

"Not still hoping for something to happen with Miss West?"

"No. I'm not sure, on reflection, that I'm entirely sorry about that, from a purely selfish point of view. I wouldn't want the girl's awful mother calling on me."

Fidelma was gloomy.

"'Course you know what people are saying? Lord Lovat's getting on and he's a sick man. That girl might be a rich widow before we know it."

Agatha tried a diamond necklace with no better results.

"I refuse even to think about that. The situation is bad enough as it is. Damn Rossmayne! Why did he have to rescue that gypsy in the first place? If he'd boxed her ears and sent her on her way Timothy wouldn't be as he is now."

"Men can be very trying."

"They're more than that." Agatha settled for a neat row of rubies. "Men are, always have been, and always will be, an infernal nuisance. What a pity we can't do without the wretches, Fiddy. How very much better off we'd be."

* * *

A week after Amsterdam left Dartmoor, Topaz told Lovat and Andrew that she was returning to Yelton. Rossmayne had come to visit Rodney, delighted with the change in the boy, but suddenly stricken when Topaz made her announcement.

"Topaz, you can't!"

"Of course she can't." Lovat snapped out the words, his face pasty and covered with sweat. "It's madness."

"I don't want to upset either of you, but I have to go. My mind is quite made up. The outbreak of scarlet fever is worse than was first thought. Quite a few have died and new cases are taken in every day."

Lovat felt his strength being sapped. He was having to spend longer and longer periods in bed, conscious of the thudding of his heart which seemed to be ticking his life away. Now his beloved Topaz was proposing to walk into a place where Death held sway.

"No, no, it's out of the question. You'd catch the plaguey thing yourself. The Sisters are there; let them tend the sick."

"Two of the Sisters have died already. They need more helpers and I'm young and strong."

"The fever takes no count of that." The marquis had also lost his colour, horrified because he knew how stubborn Topaz could be. "Think of Rodney."

"He's in good hands. Andrew, Oswin, this is something I

have to do. Please try to understand. Since I was married I have thought of no one but myself."

"That isn't true. You've looked after me."

"Dear Oswin, you haven't needed much of my tending. I have done what I wanted to do, enjoyed a season in London, have been dressed in fine clothes and jewels." She paused, embracing the two men with one glance. "And I have loved as I wanted to love. Now I must pay God what I owe Him."

"But not this way!" Andrew was desperate as he saw her hardening resolve. "Topaz, my dear, not this way."

"This is the way God has chosen for me. It is clear to me, if not to you. Oswin, I would like to go with your blessing."

"I beseech you to think again. I know what you've been trying to say, but this –"

The argument continued for a further ten minutes, at the end of which Lovat was exhausted and Rossmayne half out of his mind.

Lovat said tiredly:

"I can't hold you back physically; wish I could."

"Then you'll let me go?"

"Reluctantly."

"I want you to agree willingly."

"You ask too much."

"Please – for me."

At last Oswin managed a small smile for her.

"Never could refuse you anything, could I? Weak, that's what I've been. Should have brought you to heel while I had more fire in me."

"Andrew?"

"It is not my place to tell you what to do."

"Andrew!" She was reproachful. "Please!"

"Very well. You have my agreement for what it's worth."

When she had gone the two men looked at each other.

"Just as wild as she was in the beginning," said Oswin sadly. "Neither the nuns nor London society have changed her one whit. We have decked her in silk and diamonds, but we haven't caged her."

The marquis looked grey.

"More's the pity."

"It's part of her charm, of course. M'dear fellow, you must know that better than anyone."

"I do, but now I'm afraid. Really afraid for the first time in my life. Dear God, Lovat. What if she doesn't come back?"

Nine

Two weeks after Topaz returned to Yelton, Horatia Manners was studying her reflection in the mirror.

She tried to pretend that she still looked as she'd done at eighteen, but a double chin and lines round her mouth and eyes laughed back at her.

She saw Nettie Connell come in with an armful of clean linen, glad to have someone to talk to. Nettie had been an invaluable ally, clever enough to get the marquis to keep her on even after the need of her services as a lady's maid appeared to be over. Connell had kept in touch through a third party, so that Horatia had known what was going on at High Brook.

The maid was also useful when Horatia felt low. Then she would talk for hours about Leinster, not hiding her grief as she spoke of her continuing love for him. Connell thought her mistress was mad to mourn for any man, particularly someone who seemed to be of no importance. But such sessions always ended with Nettie receiving money, or a trinket, or an unwanted gown, together with an assurance that she was a tower of strength. It fed her vanity to be the marchioness's confidante. Such a thing had never happened to her before and she intended to hold on to her post at whatever cost.

She was slightly put out when the marchioness was evasive over the removal of Rodney. She had obeyed Horatia to the letter concerning the boy's treatment, making sure his nursemaid had done the same. Then, quite suddenly, he was gone, taken off to live with Lord and Lady Lovat.

She had probed delicately, but Horatia always changed the subject. She was determined to get at the truth one day, little knowing that her mistress was equally set on keeping the facts from her.

Connell had not been with Horatia at the time she was having an affair with Charles Beckwith. The marchioness used her maid, but she had no illusions about her. Nettie's main interest was her own well-being and fortunes. To let slip the reason why the gypsy had got her own way was to put a lethal weapon in Connell's hand and Horatia knew it. Nettie would betray anyone if there was enough money in it for her.

Since her passage of arms with Topaz, Horatia's hatred of the girl had grown stronger with each day that passed. She had made plan after plan to pay the Lovat woman back for what she had done, and the threat she had posed, but it always came back to Purvis, Lovat's valet.

As Nettie crossed the room and opened the cupboard, Horatia had no idea that her embittered prayers were about to be answered.

"Heard about Purvis, m'lady? You know, Lord Lovat's man. Quite a figure hereabouts he was. Much thought of."

The marchioness raised her head, meeting her reflection again. The blood had receded from her cheeks, her eyes quite blank.

"Was?"

"Aye. He were out last evening taking a ride up Cap Tor. Seems the mist came down out of nowhere and the horse took fright. Threw him right out of the saddle, snapping his neck like a twig." Suddenly Nettie saw her mistress's face. "M'lady? Did I upset you? I'm sorry if – "

"No, no, it's not that." The marchioness turned to look at her maid. "Nettie, I can trust you, can't I?"

"No need to ask. I'd have thought you'd have had proof enough of that."

"I'm sorry, don't be angry. It's just that this is so important."

Connell was mollified by her mistress's anxiety.

"Of course, m'lady. What is it?"

"It's about Purvis."

Nettie folded her hands and waited. It sounded interesting.

"Yes?"

"Well, he found out something about me – something which happened when I was young and foolish. He told Lady Lovat about it. It wasn't really such a dreadful thing, but it would have distressed the marquis if it had come out. For his sake, I had to agree when that woman said she wanted to take Rodney, and after all, Rossmayne had given his consent."

Nettie pursed her lips, weighing things up. First, she wasn't to be told what Purvis had known; secondly, whatever it was it was a good deal more serious than her ladyship made out. It didn't matter. There were rich pickings in this sort of intrigue and that was what concerned Nettie most. One small point needed to be cleared up before the bargaining began.

"But that tinker could still go to his lordship if she knows what Purvis knew, that is, if she wanted to make fresh demands on you."

"He was a witness, she wasn't. It would be her word against mine and I've no doubt who'd be believed. Without him, there's no proof. I've never let anyone get the better of me yet, and I'm not going to start now. With that man dead, I'll deal with Topaz Lovat as she deserves."

The two women exchanged a long look. Each knew where the other stood now and it was time to get down to business.

"What had you in mind, m'lady?"

"That depends on how much help you'll give me."

Nettie examined the ties of her lawn apron.

"Value for value, ma'm?"

The marchioness let her breath go. Connell was hooked.

"Of course, as always."

"What's the plan?"

"To reunite Rodney with Lady Lovat."

Connell's eyes flew to her mistress's face again.

"But she's at –"

"Precisely."

There was another pause.

"I've always fancied owning one of those cottages up by Dean Tor," said Connell, sure of herself now. "Nice little places."

"Why not?" Horatia was reeling in her catch. "Very sensible, Nettie. One should always have property if one can. And you can."

"Very grateful, m'lady. I'd need a small income for its upkeep."

"Naturally." That settled, Horatia turned to the main issue. "The question is how to get hold of the boy."

It was Connell's turn to oblige.

"Now there I can help you. Just so happens I've a friend working for Lord Lovat, a Bessy Green. She wanted to be the boy's nursemaid but she were passed over for Amy Parks. She's been watching Parks, hoping to catch her at some mischief so she'll be sent packing."

"And?"

"Every afternoon when his lordship takes his nap and the staff are below stairs, Parks takes Master Rodney to the stables. She's got a sweetheart; one of the younger grooms. Bessy kept watch on them for a while, but the pattern never changed. Master Rodney plays outside or in the little copse close by. Madam Parks is inside one of the stables doing goodness knows what. Bessy's just biding her time, but she's away just now, visiting her sick mother."

"Could you get him?"

"Reckon so. When?"

"Very soon."

"And when I've got him?"

"Gag him and wrap him in a blanket and bring him to where I'll have a carriage some half mile away. Then I'll drive you to Yelton. You can hand him over to the Sisters and tell them he's got scarlet fever. He may not have it at the time, but he soon will have."

Connell considered the danger that she might contract the disease herself, measuring it against the satisfaction of owning a house and having a regular income over and above her wages. She nodded.

"Why not to-morrow?"

"Why not indeed? Well, Lady Lovat, you were so anxious to have the boy, so you can't grumble if he joins you. I wish you joy of each other. God damn you both!"

* * *

Topaz worked long hours in the barn which Oswin's money had built. Every square inch had been given over to the straw beds on which the patients lay. Even the chapel had been sacrificed and the Sisters had turned over their tiny quarters to the worst cases.

A rough fence had been erected some distance from the hut. To this barrier came villagers, either seeking news of their relatives or bringing new cases to hand over to the Order. None ventured into the no-man's-land between the crooked staves and the makeshift hospital save the nuns and Topaz. Food and other supplies were thrown to them and once a week Mother Benedicta and two or three of the Sisters came from the Mother House to see how bad the situation was.

The sick lay shivering, complaining of weariness, headaches, sickness and sore throats. Many of the children had fits of convulsions and all had pulses beating very rapidly as the illness progressed.

The rash started on the face, the sides of the neck, and the chest, but soon it spread all over the body. When the scarlet flush began to fade, the victims started to shed their skin. In some cases the flakes were small; in others the areas were large, like a hand slipping out of a glove or a foot pulling free of a stocking. It was this stage which Topaz found so distressing to watch, but she never let her patients see that.

Quite a number had brain disturbances and lay muttering in delirium. Others developed kidney and heart trouble; some suffered from a disease of the ear.

The Sisters went from pallet to pallet, bathing sore limbs, giving sips of water and a kindly word of encouragement. When a patient died, everything was burnt and a new bed came from the Mother House to take its place.

Topaz hardly had time to think, for she was rushed off her feet, but she shewed no signs of getting the fever herself. Sister Beatrice's iron regime of cleanliness and hygiene helped to protect those who risked their own lives for the villagers.

Then came the day when someone threw a stone over the fence with a note wrapped round it. It was taken to Topaz at once, for her name was inscribed on the outside of the paper.

She swayed on her feet and in a second Mother Benedicta was at her elbow.

"My dear, what is it? Are you unwell? Are you hot and have you – "

"Mother, it's Rodney."

Benedicta had heard all about Rodney, glad for the child's sake that a change had been made, but wary about the effect on the relationship between Topaz and the marquis.

"What about Rodney?"

"He's disappeared."

Benedicta frowned.

"You mean he's wandered off somewhere? I wouldn't

worry too much; children are always doing that."

"No, no, he's been gone for some time and a thorough search is being made. I can't leave here; I may be infectious. But I must get a message through to Andrew."

Imperceptibly, something in Benedicta withdrew.

"He will know by now."

Topaz turned her head.

"How can you be sure?"

"Because he is the boy's father. Lord Lovat will have informed him."

That pulled Topaz up short and she read what was in Benedicta's eyes.

"Yes of course, Mother. I'm afraid I panicked. It's just that I'm so tired."

"You must be. You have worked so hard and you don't have to be here at all."

"You know that I do."

The Mother Superior smiled.

"Yes, perhaps I do. Go and rest for an hour and get a cool drink. Don't fret about Rodney. The marquis will find him, you may be sure of that."

When Lovat's frantic message reached him, Andrew's first thought was about the death of Purvis. Why this should have been his immediate reaction he had no idea, but a suspicion slipped into his mind and he couldn't rid himself of it no matter how hard he tried.

Topaz had said that the dead man knew something about Horatia which she wouldn't want voiced abroad. Since Horatia had lived a somewhat scandalous existence, not caring a fig about what people thought, it had to be something serious. And now Purvis would never be able to speak of it.

He wanted to rush into Horatia's room and accuse her outright of taking Rodney, for he was certain that she had something to do with it. She had called Rodney a bastard and had wanted to throw him out. Then, later, she had been forced to stop bullying the child and let him go. She would be vindictive and unforgiving. But he had to move carefully with her, for she would only deny her complicity. The search for the boy had had to be called off as dusk came because fog had enshrouded the Moor.

It was just possible that the child had simply strayed too far from home and would be found in the morning when, if they were lucky, the brisk October winds would have blown the mist away.

The marquis didn't think this very likely but until he was sure he had to move with caution as far as Horatia was concerned. This was the time for testing her reaction, not twisting her arm behind her back until she screamed out the truth.

He found her dressing for dinner, quite fetching for once in cream sarcenet, trimmed with lace.

Horatia was smugly satisfied with the success of her plan. Bessy Green's information had been very accurate and when Rodney had ventured into the copse, Nettie had clapped a hand over his mouth and dragged him away.

The rest had been just as simple. She and Connell had met no one on their journey to Yelton and, once at the fence, the bundle of blankets was quickly passed into the arms of a waiting nun.

Their luck held when they returned. No one had seen them enter High Brook. The servants had been in their own quarters; Andrew had been out. As far as anyone knew, neither she nor Connell had left the house that afternoon.

She looked at Andrew's strained face, a warm satisfaction glowing within her. Nettie had just told her that the search had had to be abandoned because of the weather. Andrew was on the rack and it shewed.

"Yes, my dear?" She was sweetness itself. "What is it?"

"Rodney is missing, but I'm sure you've heard that."

Her exclamation was a work of art.

"Oh no! Connell, why didn't you tell me?"

Nettie played her part with equal skill.

"You were resting when it were first found the lad had

gone, m'lady. I've been trying to think of some way to tell you without upsetting you."

"But what could have happened to him? Andrew, did he run off, do you think?"

The marquis was watching his wife intently, waiting for the slightest slip of the tongue or glimmer of an expression which would give her away.

"It's possible, but there is an alternative. I suppose you know nothing about it?"

Horatia looked at Rossmayne, her blank surprise worthy of a performance by Sarah Siddons.

"I? Why of course not. How could I?"

The marquis held her gaze for a long time, but he could see she wasn't going to weaken and he turned to Nettie.

"And you, Connell? Where were you this afternoon?"

Nettie put on a show of indignation, but Horatia said smoothly:

"She was here with me; we were altering a gown. Really, Andrew, how can you be so cruel as to suggest that we would harm a small boy?"

"You harmed him once before," he said curtly and walked to the door. "I hope he's found to-morrow, Horatia, because if he isn't, you and I are going to have another talk."

In his room, the marquis paced the floor trying to think what it was which was bothering him so much about Purvis and Horatia. It was an elusive worry which floated just out of reach, like the tail-end of a dream which slips away upon awakening.

Then at last the answer came to him, as chill and fearful as the fog outside. Topaz and Oswin knew something about Horatia because they had been told about it by Purvis. Purvis knew something because he'd actually seen whatever it was. He had been the dangerous one. It had to be that; there was no other explanation.

Horatia wasn't afraid of Lovat, or Topaz, or of hearsay. It had been Purvis who had frightened her into giving Rodney up. Now Purvis had gone and couldn't bear witness against her. Once she knew that the valet was dead, Horatia had begun her revenge. Andrew had never been surer of anything in his life.

Horatia had hated Rodney and now the boy whom she had called a bastard had suddenly vanished from the face of the earth.

* * *

It was several hours before Topaz came across Rodney. She had been working at one end of the hospital, whilst the child had been laid on a bed in what had once been the Sisters' quarters.

"I know how weary you are," said Sister Beatrice when she encountered Topaz bringing in some fresh water. "But there are a few children in the rear rooms. Sister Cecilia admitted them, but I'm afraid we haven't had much chance to look at them for an hour or two. Three more men have died and six new cases have come in. The poor mites will be frightened. Have you the strength left to go and see them?"

"Of course." Topaz was glad of the crippling work-load. It helped to stop her thinking of Rodney and what could have happened to him. She knew Oswin and Andrew would have instituted a search, but it was dark and misty and probably they'd had to give up until the morning.

She moved quietly between the beds, hearing the moans and sighs which meant death was near. A short walk in the swirling fog and she was at her old hut, opening the door softly so as not to startle the children.

The first was a girl of six, her face a brilliant red, her eyes terrified. Topaz was very gentle as she dabbed cooling water on the hot little cheeks, murmuring words of comfort before passing on to the next pallet.

At the fourth bed the occupant appeared to be tightly wrapped in a blanket, hardly moving at all. She pulled the coverings aside, words of reassurance on her lips, when two familiar eyes met her own.

She didn't know how she managed to stay conscious. The floor was rocking, the ceiling falling in on her. Then she managed to steady herself, her parched lips mouthing words in a whisper.

"Rodney! What are you doing here?"

He shook his head, throwing his arms about Topaz's neck.

"Don't know." His voice was breaking. "Someone took me away."

"Who, darling, who?"

"Didn't see. I'm glad you've come. I'm frightened."

She held him close for a minute or two and then fetched Sister Beatrice. The latter made a thorough examination of Rodney and shook her head.

"No, no sign of the fever but he's at risk here, you know that?"

"Of course and we can't let him go." Topaz was desperate. "Isn't there somewhere we could put him away from the others?"

"You know as well as I do that there isn't a square inch left. And he's been with the other children for several hours. All we can do is to ask God for his mercy."

"And send word to the marquis and my husband."

"Not to-night. The fog is too thick. Sister Martha's just come back from the fence. There's no one there."

"But to wait so long."

"I know, I know, but there's nothing we can do."

As soon as it was light, Topaz went to the fence. A few had gathered there, some bringing food, others carrying new sufferers to the hospital.

Quickly, Topaz chose her messenger. He was a young man, Cooper by name, strong and sturdy, who had helped the nuns by chopping wood and carrying water. He nodded at once and ran off to where his old pack-horse was tethered.

Andrew went cold as he listened to Cooper. Shock and

fear was followed by towering rage, for Rodney's appearance in the fever compound could have been no accident. He went straight to Horatia, accusing her outright that time, threatening her with violence if she didn't tell the truth.

She remained as steady as a rock as his wrath pounded against her.

"You are insane," she said when at last his fury was spent. "Do you seriously suggest I would risk my life by taking that worthless brat into a district where there's scarlet fever?"

"Someone could have taken him for you. And how was he removed from Stone Towers?"

"I haven't the faintest idea. Why don't you ask him now you know where he is?"

"I shall," he returned bleakly, "and if the boy is able to furnish me with the facts I want, then, Horatia, your life which is so precious to you won't be worth a moment's purchase."

Horatia remained unmoved, secure in the knowledge that there wasn't the slightest shred of evidence against her.

"He won't accuse me because I'm quite innocent of the charge. Look elsewhere, Rossmayne. You'll never prove anything as far as I'm concerned."

"Not as Purvis could have done?" he asked and had the satisfaction of seeing every drop of blood drain out of her cheeks. "We'll see, Horatia, we'll see."

But at the fence he got no help. He called to Topaz to question Rodney, but she gestured to him that she couldn't hear. He scribbled a note and threw it as far as he could, but Topaz couldn't return a like missive for fear of contagion.

All she could do was to shake her head to indicate that Rodney knew nothing and Andrew turned away sick at heart, hoping against hope that the girl he loved, and his son, would not fall prey to the dreadful scourge which was claiming so many lives.

Later that day Mother Benedicta arrived and sent for Topaz.

"I'm sorry to hear what has happened, my dear. It is a most dreadful thing and whoever is responsible is an instrument of the Devil. How is Rodney?"

"Still without the fever." Topaz was very white, her hands clenched together to stop them shaking. "He doesn't know what happened to him; he didn't see who took him. The marquis was here, but I'm not sure whether I made him understand that. Poor Oswin; he will be so dreadfully unhappy. I wonder if he's got my message yet. Yes, he must have. If Andrew got his, my husband will know, too."

"It's about Lord Lovat that I've come to see you. Sit down, Topaz."

Topaz turned dazed eyes to the Mother Superior.

"You've come here – about Oswin? Why? What's happened?"

"Do as I say. Sit down."

"No, no, I can't. Tell me, Mother; please tell me. What's wrong with Oswin?"

Benedicta watched Topaz with concern. The girl was on the verge of a breakdown. Too much hard labour, too much of death, the shock of the boy being brought into the hospital. It wasn't surprising that Topaz was at the end of her tether. Now she, Benedicta, had more bad news for her.

"When he was told what had happened, Lord Lovat had a stroke."

"Oh no! You mean he's dead?"

"No, but he's very ill. You must prepare yourself for his passing, although this may not come for a few weeks."

"What did he say?"

Benedicta took Topaz's hands in hers, squeezing them gently.

"He can't speak or move."

When Topaz fainted, Mother Benedicta called to two of the Sisters to help her to get the girl into the fresh air. The nuns sponged her ashen face, ready with a cup of water when Topaz came round.

"How stupid," she said as she looked up at Benedicta. "I've never done that before in my whole life."

"You've never been in such a situation as this. It's not to be wondered at. You'll be all right in a moment. Just rest for a while. Thank you, Sisters, you may go back to your work."

After a minute or two Topaz said slowly:

"This is my punishment, you know."

Benedicta said nothing, waiting for Topaz to go on.

"God is making me pay for marrying without love, but poor Oswin is suffering the most from His wrath. I left the convent and had such a wonderful time in London. So many new clothes and jewels when people here in Yelton were going hungry. This is the price I'm paying for my fine feathers."

"I doubt it. Clothes and jewellery are not particularly sinful even if other things are."

Topaz gave a shuddering sigh.

"You are talking about the marquis, aren't you? Yes, I expect that's the real reason why this has happened. I shouldn't have loved him, but I did. I still do. And I went to bed with him, just once."

"I thought perhaps that was so. Ask God for forgiveness and I will pray for you. Our Father is much more merciful than you give Him credit for. Have you any idea how Rodney got here?"

"Yes, I think I know who was behind it but, even if I live to go home again, I'll never be able to prove it. Mother, don't waste prayers on me, I'm not worth it. Pray that Rodney will stay well; I beg you, pray that Andrew's son may live."

Ten

On the morning when Mother Benedicta went to see Topaz, Timothy Amsterdam returned home.

He was horrified to hear what had happened in his absence, appalled to learn that neither Andrew nor Oswin had been able to stop Topaz from going to Yelton.

"No one could stop her," said Lady Agatha. "She just wouldn't listen to either of them. Andrew called on me and explained how hard he and Lovat had tried. She's pig-headed that gypsy, but by God she's got courage. Now her husband's near to death and Andrew's son is locked up with all those fever patients. Yes, Fiddy, what is it?"

Fidelma came panting into the room, her cap awry, her cheeks pink with exertion.

"I've just seen Mrs. Rouse."

Agatha raised her eyebrows.

"I don't know who Mrs. Rouse is, but I hardly think she will prove to be of interest to me. Go away, I'm trying to tell my nephew of the tragedies which have befallen us."

"Nothing's befallen you," retorted Fidelma with more truth than tact. "And Mrs. Rouse will interest you very much when you hear what I've got to say."

Agatha made an impatient gesture.

"All right, all right, get on with it. What about this woman, Rouse?"

"Her daughter went to Yelton yesterday; 'er young man's gone and got the fever, poor feller. She was takin' him some food, stuff that he likes, see?"

"Yes, yes, go on."

"Well, Mrs. Rouse's daughter, May, was at the fence

they put up to keep people away from the hospital. While she was there a woman came up and handed over what looked to May like a big blanket, but the Sister who took it said: 'Poor child, poor child,' so it must have been a little 'un."

"I've never known anyone take so long to tell a story as you. Do get to the point."

"Right, I will. The woman who handed the youngster over was Nettie Connell, the marchioness's maid. May knows her quite well and she saw Connell's face when her hood fell back, and who would the child be but – "

"She wouldn't." Agatha was gripping the arms of her chair. "Even Horatia Manners wouldn't do that. Timothy? Where are you going?"

Amsterdam turned at the door.

"I have something to do, Aunt Ag."

Agatha felt a frisson run down her spine, trying desperately to stop him without shewing her anxiety.

"But you've only just come in."

"I know, but this can't wait."

"Be careful, Timothy."

He gave Agatha a loving smile.

"I always am, but thank you for caring."

As soon as he had gone Agatha grabbed Fidelma's arm.

"Run down to the stables and get one of the grooms – Barker would be best, I think – to follow Timothy, but tell him to keep out of sight. I don't like this. At first when Timothy heard our bad news he was just angry, which was to be expected. But when you spoke of Connell I saw the look in his eyes. It was – oh, never mind. Hurry woman, hurry, or Barker will lose track of him."

"What's Barker to do when he catches up with Mr. Timothy?"

"It depends what Timothy is doing. Tell him to use his common sense.

"Oh, Fiddy, Fiddy, what do you think Timothy is planning to do?"

* * *

On his way to High Brook, Amsterdam met Honor West. He tried to hurry past her with a polite word, but she was determined to have her say.

He scarcely heard her proposition, blurted out in a voice hoarse with emotion, realizing he had missed something of great importance to her when he saw her eyes fill with tears.

"I'm sorry, Honor. I've much on my mind just now. What did you say?"

"I said that we could be companions, you and I. I know you don't love me, but I love you so much it would make up for that. I'll do everything in my power to make you happy, I truly will. And I won't care that you want Lady Lovat, I promise."

Amsterdam was torn between a raging desire not to waste time and compassion for the girl who was waiting for his answer.

"It wouldn't work, Honor, and I think you know that. It would be a calamity for both of us. You have the whole world before you. Find someone who can make you happy."

"The whole world means nothing to me without you, and only you could make me happy."

She ran away from him, rather ungainly as she got into the saddle and rode off to the north. Timothy shook his head. Even if such an arrangement as Honor envisaged had been acceptable to him, it was too late now.

About half a mile from Yelton Honor drew rein and looked ahead to where the convent's outpost lay. Lady Lovat had given up her safe and comfortable existence to nurse the sick and dying, knowing she might never leave the place alive.

Honor dismounted and walked a few paces nearer. It was one way out for her. She could try to be as valorous as Topaz Lovat and do something worthwhile with her life. It was all over with Timothy now, for she had been bold enough to put her proposal to him and had it turned down flat.

The alternative was home, mother, and Mr. George

Chambers, who still shewed no sign of giving up the chase.

Suddenly she felt as if a huge weight had been lifted from her and she slapped Barty, her roan, on his rump, sending him racing off in high dudgeon. Her feet skimmed over the ground until she reached the palisade, clambering over it and ignoring the warning cries of those who waited there.

A small and very grand old lady, wearing the habit of the Sisters of St. Francis, emerged from one of the huts. Honor hesitated, but only for a moment. She had already burnt her boats and she walked up to the aged nun, giving a polite bob, for it seemed appropriate.

"I'm Honor West," she said, trying to get her breath back. "I hope you don't mind but I've come to see what I can do for you. I don't know anything about nursing, but I can learn. Even if I can't help the sick, I can wash, scrub floors and cook, that is, if there's any food."

Mother Benedicta considered Honor carefully.

"You understand the dangers?" she asked eventually. "Our helpers die as well as the villagers."

"I realize that. I still want to join you."

"Are you running to us, or away from something else?"

Honor held her head high. This was no time for lying.

"I'm running away from something else, but please don't turn me down because of that. I could have gone anywhere, but I came here. Perhaps it was meant to be."

Benedicta inclined her head.

"Very well. I shan't ask for further reasons. Serve God as best you can. Even the blessed saints can't do more than that."

* * *

Andrew wasn't in when Timothy reached High Brook and he was glad of it. It wasn't Rossmayne he wanted to see and his enquiry made to one of the grooms was very casual.

"'Er ladyship, sir? Why, she's gone to Yellowmead Down to see some friends of 'ers. Regular visitor to the Wentworths, she is."

"I'd like to meet her on her return journey." A few coins changed hands. "Which route does she normally take on the way home?"

Timothy listened to the groom, thanked him, and mounted up again.

After a few miles he realized how dark it had grown and there were sinister grey wisps curling like feathers in the air. He went on, listening for the sound of another rider.

He managed to pick up the track which Horatia usually used and waited, quite still as the fog thickened about him. When he heard the sound of hooves, he bent down to pat his horse's neck.

"Don't be frightened, Beau. It's just another traveller like ourselves."

Horatia saw Timothy and pulled up abruptly.

"Good God, Timothy, I thought you were a phantom. I imagined I was the only one reckless enough to chance a ride home through this weather. I was told you were in London."

"I got back to-day."

"I can't think why you bothered. This is a dull, ghastly place. I wish Rossmayne would move to town for good. What are you doing here anyway?"

"Waiting for you."

There was something in Amsterdam's tone which made Horatia's smile fade.

"Are you being chivalrous?"

"No."

"Then why have you come?"

"To talk about a brave woman and a small boy. Oh, and about Connell, your maid, as well."

Horatia's jaw hardened.

"By a brave woman I suppose you mean that gypsy. We all know how you feel about her. What a dolt you are to eat your heart out for a nobody like that."

"Just as Andrew does."

"What!"

The marchioness went rigid, her shock genuine. Timothy smiled caustically.

"You didn't know? How odd. I thought Connell knew everything about everyone, but then Andrew and Topaz have always been very discreet, unlike you."

"Are you saying that Andrew is in love with that girl? I don't believe it."

"It's perfectly true and she returns his feelings. Poor Horatia, how out of touch you are."

"You're making it up."

"Why should I? What would I have to gain by such a lie? They're in love, Horatia, believe me. Now about Rodney and Connell. She was seen, you know. Someone recognized her when she was at the fence. Careless of her, wasn't it? You would have been more careful if you'd gone yourself, but you were afraid of catching the fever so you sent Connell instead.

"You tried to kill Andrew's son, damn you! You heartless, evil bitch. You tried to kill a helpless child and break Lady Lovat's heart in so doing."

Horatia didn't waste any time pleading ignorance or innocence. There was something in Amsterdam's manner which was wholly different from Andrew's angry enquiries and accusations. Timothy hadn't even raised his voice, but his eyes were terrible to see.

She slid from the saddle and began to run, but the fog caught her up in its greedy arms and she staggered as she fell over some clitter, leaving the path and safety.

Slowly Timothy dismounted, following in the direction which the marchioness had taken. When he heard her scream he tied Beau's reins to a tree and gave him one last caress.

"You'll have a rotten night, old boy," he said as the horse rubbed against him. "But it'll be all right in the morning. Someone will find you then. Yes, everything will be all right by then."

Horatia's muffled screams were growing louder and more anguished.

"Help me, for God's sake, help me! I'm in a mire and I can't get a foothold. The filthy stuff's up to my knees already. Timothy! Can't you hear me?"

Amsterdam picked his way carefully over the clitter and left the footpath, moving down to the place from which the marchioness's shrieks were coming. He waded out into the deadly bog, hearing the dreadful suck which was the source of its power.

"It's all right, Horatia," he said calmly. "I'm going to take your hand and hold it fast. Come, there's nothing for you to worry about now. I'm here and I'm going to stay with you. Oh, my dear, how very foolish you were to run."

* * *

Lady Agatha was in her drawing-room, sitting as upright as a guardsman. Every hair was in place, but her face was like a piece of bleached calico. Fidelma was behind her, holding a shawl which Agatha had twice rejected. Even the maid's fresh colour had gone and her fingers were busy pleating her mistress's wrap.

Andrew stood by the fire, still frozen by the news which Agatha had given him when he obeyed her summons to call upon her without delay.

The door opened and the thick-set figure of Barker, Lady Agatha's chief groom, appeared. The man had been given a chance to change into dry clothes and have a stiff grog. After all, there was no longer any need to hurry.

"Ah, Barker." Agatha was supremely controlled, centuries of breeding and self-discipline behind her as she nodded to her servant. "I want you to tell the marquis exactly what you told me earlier.

"I have explained that I instructed you to follow my nephew. Just go on from there."

Barker was feeling queasy. He had been very fond of Mr. Timothy and what he had seen would have turned the stomach of any man. He didn't know how the old girl could sit there so unmoved. When he had first arrived home she had shewn something approaching indifference. She seemed even more detached now, as if they were discussing some quite ordinary things, like growing climbing roses over an arched trellis.

"Yes, m'lady." Barker looked at the marquis and hadn't the slightest idea how to begin. "Well – I – "

"It's all right, Barker." Rossmayne had a rather better notion of how to deal with the Barkers of this world than Agatha. "No need for you to worry. Just use your own words; there's plenty of time."

"Thank you, m'lord." Barker wiped his forehead with a red handkerchief, summoning up enough courage to recall the facts as he remembered them. "Well, like I told 'er ladyship, I tracked Mr. Timothy to High Brook and then on to the path which leads to the main road to Yellowmead Down. I was quiet, like, so 'e didn't 'ear me. Then 'e stopped and so did I. It were growin' dark and the mist was up to its tricks again. Thick as a blanket one minute, then blowin' off for a whiles so one could see ahead."

"And then?" The marquis was patient. The man had had a bad experience. "What happened after that?"

"Then I 'eard another rider comin' and after that, voices. I got off old Jack and tied 'im up, so as I could get a bit nearer. It were the marchioness, m'lord, talking to Mr. Timothy."

"Could you hear what they were saying?" Andrew hoped fervently that the man hadn't, for Agatha's sake if for no one else's.

"No, not a word. Weren't enough cover to get that close."

Andrew said a silent prayer of thanksgiving.

"Please go on."

"Well, all of a sudden like, the marchioness gets off 'er horse and begins to run. When Mr. Timothy dismounted, I was able to move up, 'cos 'is back were turned to me. The fog were thicker, too. Couldn't see me 'and in front of me face. Then she begins to scream. Gawd, I've never 'eard the likes of them screams afore, beggin' your pardon, sir."

Andrew waved the apology aside and Barker dabbed at his brow again.

"She were in the old Belrow Mire. Not many bogs on Dartmoor are dangerous, m'lord, as well you know, but that one is. I started to run as best I could, 'er ladyship still cryin' out to Mr. Timothy to save 'er. She said she were sinkin' and couldn't find no firm ground."

Agatha was looking straight in front of her, taking no notice of those about her. The groom shot her an uneasy look, but decided to get the rest off his chest as soon as possible.

"It were like bein' blind, but I don't need to tell your lordship what a moorland fog is like. I kept on in the direction of the cries and then I saw I was on the edge of the mire myself. I jumped back and it was then that the mist rolled away as if a giant had given it a great big puff. I saw – that is – I saw – "

"Yes?" Andrew was trying to ignore the dull throbbing inside him which was the beginning of his mourning for Timothy. "What did you see?"

"Just their 'ands and arms – one of each. That is to say, one of 'er ladyship's and one of Mr. Timothy's. 'Is fingers were tight round 'er wrist like a vice, as if 'e'd been tryin' to pull 'er out. But there weren't no chance of that. They were both too close to the centre of the bog."

"What did you do? Did you do anything?"

"I got 'old of a bit o' branch." Barker's face was crumpled with grief. "But it weren't no good 'cos they couldn't see it. Only their 'ands were above the surface and then they were gorn as well and there weren't nothin' left."

For a moment, Barker's voice faded from Andrew's consciousness. He was back at Foxton Mire with Timothy. He could hear his own words ringing in his ears. 'It was a terrible way to die,' he had said. But Horatia hadn't died that time, and his pity had been wasted. Now it was different. Horatia's ruse had become a reality, but it was still a terrible end for a human being. Then he returned to the present, reassuring Barker.

"No, I see. I'm sorry, Barker. No reproach was intended. As you say, there was nothing anyone could have done."

Barker scuttled out as soon as the word was given and Andrew kissed Agatha's hand.

"I'll come back later," he said gently. "I have things to do, but I won't leave you alone too long."

Agatha watched him go, then snapped her fingers.

"I'll have that shawl now, woman, unless you've creased it to bits."

Fidelma tucked it round the frail shoulders, patting it into position.

"There, there, that's better. Nice and cosy now, aren't we?"

"You ought to be some luckless child's nanny. Stop treating me as if I were three years old."

"Sometimes you behave as if you were three years old."

"I'll get rid of you, you insolent – insolent – Dear God! Do you really think Timothy went into that mire to help Horatia Manners?"

Fidelma had been conjuring with the same thought since she had first heard Barker's tale, but she said stoutly:

"We'll never know, will we? Barker will tell everyone that Mr. Timothy died a hero. Best left that way, don't you think?"

The iron control was cracking at last as Agatha laid her head against Fidelma's broad chest.

"But what am I going to do without him? Whatever am I going to do without my dear boy?"

"First you'll have a good cry. I always says there's nothing like a good cry to cheer you up. Then we'll both have a brandy."

"You're Irish right enough, you old fool. Fiddy, Fiddy, hold me!"

Fidelma O'Brien drew the small body into her arms,

rocking it back and forth.

"That I will, mavourneen, that I will. And I'll say some prayers for Mr. Timothy whilst I'm doing it.

"Oh, my poor little colleen. What a bad day you've had, to be sure. What a very bad day it's been."

* * *

Two months later Topaz returned home. The fever had burnt itself out, death having gathered lives as industriously as a farmer gathered wheat at harvest time.

She looked down at Oswin with tears in her eyes. He was so still, like a figure made of wax. Just the dribble from the corner of his mouth and the faint heartbeat indicating that his hour had not yet come.

"My dear." Topaz took one of the stiff hands in hers. "I don't know whether you can hear me, but I hope you can. I did love you. Not as I love Andrew, but you knew that. Yet it was love just the same. I wanted to do so much to repay you for all your kindness to me, but now I'll never be able to. Dearest Oswin; I'll never forget you, never."

Then she went downstairs to where Andrew was waiting for her. Curtis and Rodney were up in the nursery with a new and stricter nursemaid. Rodney, like Topaz, hadn't caught scarlet fever and he had come back as lively as a cricket and full of devilment.

"Any change?"

Topaz shook her head.

"No and there won't be. He'll be like that until he dies."

"Does the doctor know how long?"

"A week or two, maybe more. No one can be certain. Andrew, I want to hear the whole story of Timothy and the way he died."

He looked at her, still weak with relief because she had been spared. She was thinner, the new slenderness giving her an almost ethereal look, the hollows under the high cheekbones making the dark eyes enormous.

"Very well. I'll tell you what Barker, that's Agatha Waring's groom, told me. That's all I know."

"Don't leave anything out. I want to hear everything."

He pulled her down beside him on the couch by the fire and when he had finished, Topaz said wearily:

"You're not sure, are you? You don't quite believe what Barker told you."

"He wasn't lying," returned the marquis quickly. "I'm sure of that."

"No, I don't suppose he was, but I can read in your eyes what you are thinking. You're wondering why they were there together, and whether Timothy went to her aid, or whether he – "

Rossmayne put his fingers over her lips.

"Don't say the words. Let it be as the groom saw it."

"Very well, but first I want to know the truth. I'm not a child and you don't have to protect me. I don't believe that Timothy met your wife by accident. Tell me why he was on the Moor that day just as she was returning from Yellowmead Down."

Andrew looked down at his hands.

"You've heard of Timothy's Aunt Agatha, of course. Her maid, Fidelma, has a friend who saw Nettie Connell hand Rodney over at the hospital fence. Connell was my wife's maid. Fidelma told her mistress what had happened whilst Timothy was present. Then he said he had something to do and left. That was the last time his aunt saw him alive."

"So he might have walked into the mire deliberately, not to save the marchioness but to – Andrew! Would he have done that?"

"I think perhaps he might, for us. But as far as the rest of the world is concerned it was an accident and Timothy died trying to save Horatia. We don't want his name blackened, do we?"

"No, of course not."

"Then never speak of this again."

She rested against his shoulder, feeling drained. She had

told Timothy not to love her too much, but he hadn't listened.

"I won't. How you will miss Timothy."

"Yes, I shall. He was part of my life."

"And part of mine in a way."

"That is over now. It's my turn to ask for an explanation, if I may. What hold did Purvis have over Horatia? You said she would never dare to harm Rodney again. She didn't dare, until Purvis was dead."

When Topaz had told him the tale he shuddered unseen. He had been right in his guess, but had never dreamt for a moment that murder had been involved.

"That is something else to forget," he said, pushing the past back where it belonged. "Tell me how things are going at Yelton. I hear that Honor West is there. I didn't think she had it in her. I hope she didn't catch the fever."

Topaz sat up, taking her cue from Andrew. Timothy was dead and nothing would bring him back. It was time to talk of other things. She didn't think it necessary to mention Honor's love for Timothy. Andrew might not have understood that once Honor's tears had dried she had said triumphantly: 'At last he is going to be mine. No one can take him away from me now.'

"No, she didn't get the fever and yes, she had the will-power to escape from her mother. I heard all about Lady West. She sounds like a dragon. Eventually, Honor will go back to the Mother House to help the Sisters there. I think her future will be a happy one."

Andrew took Topaz's face between his hands as he'd done once before.

"And what of us, my darling? Is our future to be happy, too?"

"I'm sure of it."

"Do you think that in about a year's time, when we have paid our tribute to Timothy and Oswin, we could get married? Would Oswin approve?"

Her eyes were bright with unshed tears.

"I know he would, but Andrew, I'm only a – "

"You are Lady Lovat and the woman I love. Before long you will be my marchioness and the mother of my two sons. I shall want more children, of course."

"Will you indeed, my lord?"

"Most certainly."

"Perhaps an afternoon spent with Curtis and Rodney may cause you to change your mind."

"I doubt that. Where shall we go after we are married? Vienna, Italy, Egypt? We'll travel wherever you like."

"Anywhere? You give me your word?"

"Yes. What outlandish place have you in mind which needs a promise in advance?"

"I want to go to our cottage," she whispered and put her arms round his neck. "For me, there is no place on earth to equal it."

He had to steady his voice before he could reply.

"Dear Topaz. Sometimes you make me want to cry."

"And at other times?"

She had thrown off her sadness for a while, gently teasing the man who held her heart.

"At other times I – never mind; I'll tell you when I'm free to do so."

"I cannot wait a year for your kiss. Andrew, I need you now."

The marquis held her at arm's length, looking at her in a way which sent a shiver through her.

"Lovat, m'dear fellow," he said finally. "I hope you'll forgive me, but I have to agree with her. A year is far too long to wait for her kiss. All right, you wanton, come here."

Just before their lips met he said very softly:

"You're not the only one who hungers, you know. My wild, brave, beautiful gypsy girl, I need you, too."

DATE DUE
